MW01193267

SURVIVOR

REED MONTGOMERY BOOK 5

LOGAN RYLES

SEVERN RIVER
PUBLISHING

Copyright © 2021 by Logan Ryles.

All rights reserved.

No part of this book may be reproduced in any form or by any electronic or mechanical means, including information storage and retrieval systems, without written permission from the author, except for the use of brief quotations in a book review.

Severn River Publishing
SevernRiverBooks.com

This is a work of fiction. Names, characters, businesses, places, events and incidents are either the products of the author's imagination or used in a fictitious manner. Any resemblance to actual persons, living or dead, or actual events is purely coincidental.

ISBN: 978-1-64875-540-8 (Paperback)

ALSO BY LOGAN RYLES

The Reed Montgomery Series

Overwatch

Hunt to Kill

Total War

Smoke and Mirrors

Survivor

Death Cycle

Sundown

The Prosecution Force Series

Brink of War

First Strike

Election Day

Failed State

To find out more about Logan Ryles and his books, visit

severnriverbooks.com/authors/logan-ryles

For my brothers

1

Gordon often marveled at how lucky he was. Some men worked because they needed to pay bills, needed the health insurance, or needed to escape bitter home lives. Other men worked for the money. Maybe they worked in the oil fields or one of the tall bank towers in downtown New Orleans. Maybe they hated their jobs but the paychecks were too tempting to refuse.

How many men were lucky enough to go to work because their most animalistic passions drove them to? Gordon didn't know, but he guessed there couldn't be many, and that made him a lucky man. Sure, he was paid and paid well. And sure, he needed the money. A cocaine habit, a penchant for fine wines, and a raging sex addiction kept him broke despite the generous paychecks. At least the sex addiction was assuaged by the nature of his work—or inflamed by it.

Two cars waited in the parking lot behind the isolated lake house when Gordon piled out of his Range Rover. At five foot flat and well over two hundred pounds, he was wheezing by the time he made it to the back porch of the home, and he kicked irritably at the napping stray dog. The mutt whined and slunk off, leaving Gordon to cast an appraising glance at the cars as he fiddled with his keys.

A Porsche 911 and a Bentley, both late models, both black, were polished to a shine under the dim glow of the moon. While the Bentley reflected a much wealthier driver, Gordon was more interested in the Porsche. Despite its beautiful curves and clean lines, the 911 was bland in the way only a rental car can be. Exotic, but subdued, as if the person driving it failed to appreciate what he was driving. Mud was splashed against the fenders, and there were smudges on the windows—the sorts of blemishes that no true car enthusiast would tolerate on such an exquisite machine.

No, the Porsche wasn't driven by a car person. It was driven by a man with so much money that he wasn't accustomed to driving at all. He was probably used to riding in long limousines in big cities all around the world. The Porsche was this man's idea of *incognito mode,* which was a further testament to how far out of touch he was. He actually thought a Porsche was a working man's car.

Both drivers were unthinkably rich, but only one of them was noteworthy. The man in the Bentley didn't care who saw him because nobody would know who he was. The man in the Porsche was more than rich—he was an icon. And for that reason, his visit to the little lake house nestled next to the brackish, stinking waters of Lake Maurepas promised him a lot more risk than the man in the Bentley.

Nevertheless, the risk was worth it. The same animalistic desires that drove Gordon to work every day also motivated this notorious man to risk everything and visit the little lake house.

Gordon understood that. He appreciated it and was very happy to take advantage of it.

The screen door swung open on rusty hinges, and Gordon stepped into a wide kitchen on the other side, fully stocked with all the required materials to keep Gordon's guests happy. Cooking utensils, pots and pans, and an oven. None of it was used, of course. The guests rarely stayed long enough to eat, and if they did, Gordon sent his assistant, Sid, into town to collect gourmet carryout. Only the best for the clients of the house by the lake.

Beyond the kitchen was a dining room and a wide-open lobby, where the two men waited, avoiding eye contact, each pretending the other wasn't there. Gordon greeted each of them by the fake names they gave him when booking their "experience," then smiled and ushered them out of the living room, down the hall, and to the large oak door that was bolted with a padlock.

Gordon unlocked the padlock and led the men ten steps down a stairway into the darkness before flipping on a light. The basement of the house was built inside two steel shipping containers, because the lakeside Louisiana soil was too soft to sustain a traditional concrete basement. The containers had been combined, and their insides finished with insulation and drywall, while their outsides were coated in industrial paint to forestall rust.

The middle of the basement consisted of a short hallway with three doors leading out of it—one on either side and one at the end. The doors on each side led to small, hotel-like rooms, each with a large bed, plush carpeting, and thick walls that made them all but soundproof.

The third door was thick, built of steel, and locked with a bolt. On the far side of it, the hallway continued, with more doors. But these weren't built of mahogany, and they didn't conceal hotel suites. They were built of steel, hiding windowless cells beyond.

Gordon ushered each man into a hotel room, smiling but remaining silent. Most of his clients preferred not to speak. It was an absurd attempt at anonymity, which was wasted on Gordon. He usually knew exactly who his clients were, or he could guess. In most cases, he didn't care. Money was money, no matter who it came from. But on occasion, Gordon booked a guest whose identity was more than noteworthy; it was valuable. Such was the case with the man in the Porsche, who now stepped into the left-hand suite without a word and began to undo his tie as Gordon closed the door.

Gordon knew exactly who he was, in spite of the carefully orchestrated fake identity the client provided. He was, in fact, the CEO of one of the largest banking corporations in the world, and his visit to the little lake house would profit Gordon a great deal more than the petty booking fees the man had paid.

Gordon lumbered back up the steps, heaving the entire way. As soon as he cleared the doorway, he snapped his fingers, and Sid appeared out of the darkness like an apparition. Gordon's assistant was skinny, pimpled, and altogether unpleasant to look at, but he was loyal, and like Gordon, he understood the animalistic appetites of their customers.

"They're ready. Bring in the escorts."

Sid slipped past Gordon without speaking, disappearing down the stairwell. Gordon wiped sweat off his lip and breathed a long sigh, then turned down the hallway and walked to the end, where a wide stairwell led upward to the second floor. He cast a wary eye into the dark corners of the hallway, more out of habit than suspicion, then gently pressed on the wooden panel beneath the stairwell. It swung back with a soft click, providing just enough room for Gordon to squeeze through.

The space on the other side was barely big enough for him. He settled onto a stool and shut the panel behind him, his fingers brushing against the sound-deadening foam that protected a casual sneeze from exposing his position. This was the most delicate part of his entire operation, the part that, if it were ever discovered, would cost him his life.

A narrow desk filled the space directly in front of him, with three computer screens lining the wall behind it. A mouse, a few joysticks, and a pair of headphones lay on the desk. He settled the headset over his flabby ears and clicked the mouse a few times. The screens came to life, filling the tiny room with a bright blue glow and revealing crystal-clear images of the two hotel rooms beneath him.

Mr. Bentley stood impatiently by his door, already fully disrobed. Gordon gave him a casual glance, then directed his attention to Mr. Porsche. A shoeless Porsche still wore his shirt and pants, but his coat and tie were neatly folded on the nightstand. He stood with his eyes closed, oblivious to the carefully hidden cameras and microphones above him, a subtle smile of impending gratification hovering around his lips.

Gordon indulged in a smile of his own. The hotel suite, unbeknownst to its occupant, was identical to a Bangkok hotel room that Mr. Porsche had stayed in four months prior while on a layover between Shanghai and Sydney. Every detail—from the wallpaper, to the nightstands, to the pattern of the carpet—had been painstakingly replicated. It was vital that absolutely nothing about this footage be traced back to the United States.

The door to the hotel suite opened. Gordon saw Sid's skinny fingers appear around the jamb, and Mr. Porsche's eyes flashed greedily. Then a third figure appeared. It was a young girl, maybe twelve years old, with raven hair and grey eyes. She was slim—almost malnourished—and her hands trembled. She was clearly of Scandinavian origin, perhaps Danish. Gordon didn't know for sure, but he was well aware of her market value.

The door clicked shut, and the girl backed against it, her lip trembling. She wore a yellow sundress, and her hair was held back in a braid—all per the client's specifications, of course. Sid had dressed her personally two hours prior.

Mr. Porsche grinned a wolfish expression. An animalistic one. He ran one hand over his mouth, then started toward the girl.

Gordon reached down to his keyboard and hit a solitary red button.

Record.

2

The room was almost pitch dark, but after hours of sitting alone, Reed could see pretty well. A security camera was mounted near the ceiling to the right of the door, with a tiny red light glimmering beneath the lens. After a while, that lonely glow felt like the sun itself, and Reed avoided looking directly at it.

Other than the camera, the chair he sat in, and the steel table he was handcuffed to, the room was empty. It had been that way for over sixteen hours.

After facing off with Gambit in the woods outside the Alabama prison, the big man that had stood next to Gambit disappeared into the trees, dragging David Montgomery with him. Another large man appeared out of the shadows, a sniper rifle cradled in one arm. Reed's shoulders slumped when he saw the rifle. He should've expected there to be a sniper.

He walked straight into the crosshairs of that weapon, completely exposed. From the moment he had seen the model car and the crimson drops of blood on the floor of David's prison cell, his tactical awareness began to fade. In hindsight, that was obviously Gambit's intention. The car, the blood, the fire alarm, the disorientation . . . it was all part of a carefully orchestrated ploy to knock Reed off balance. To make him negotiable.

Reed twisted his wrists in the handcuffs. Had he been manipulated? Maybe. But some things couldn't be faked. David was *there*, right in front of him. Reed had seen the gleam in his eyes when David recognized his son. He saw the momentary flash of excitement and fatherly love.

And what about the car? Gambit could have pulled some old records and discovered that David Montgomery owned a 1969 Camaro Z/28, Rally Green with white stripes. Probably anyone could dig that up, but Gambit couldn't know the extreme significance of that car to David or Reed, or the relationship they shared. Gambit couldn't know how many hours the two of them spent tinkering under the hood or cruising back roads together.

Gambit couldn't have planted the toy car. David must have kept it in his cell, a memento of his past, and his son. And if David kept the toy, that could only mean his mind wasn't completely gone. Not yet. There was still something to be saved.

Reed's hands began to tremble as he thought about it. He clenched his fingers, pushing back the pain and the memories and focusing instead on the moment at hand. Leaving that prison and walking away from Banks and into the clutches of his enemies should've been a lot harder than it was. It should've broken him. But it didn't. In fact, it was the easiest decision he had made in weeks.

Banks would be safe now, protected from his private war by distance and ignorance. Meanwhile, he was closer to David than ever before. He could rescue him, restore his mind, and find out what he knew. There would be plenty of time to crush his own enemies after he saved his father.

Footsteps tapped from beyond the door. Reed kept his eyes closed, bracing himself against a flash of unwelcome light. It made sense—Gambit would want to keep him disoriented and knocked off balance. Why else had he left Reed imprisoned for so long? It was a game.

A chess move, Reed thought. Was Gambit a chess man? Did that explain the curious pseudonym? It had to be a pseudonym. Nobody names their kid *Gambit*.

The door groaned open, but there was no flood of light. Reed waited a moment, then heard the door shut. He was surprised to see Gambit standing in the dark with both hands crammed into his pockets. There was no trace of malice in his expression, and he didn't approach the table.

"Glad you're still with us," Gambit said.

Reed held up both hands and shook them, rattling the long chain of the handcuffs.

Gambit smirked.

"Come on now, Reed. The man who escaped federal prison and vanished like a ghost shouldn't be challenged by a mere pair of handcuffs."

"I had a little help back then," Reed said. His voice was toneless. None of the rage he felt against Gambit—the man who held his father—crept out of his carefully crafted facade. Maintaining control of himself was the first step in attaining control of the entire situation.

Gambit leaned against the door and shoved his hands deeper into his pockets. "So you did. Enfield, right? That's kind of his move. Or *was* his move, I should say. Pluck a killer out of prison, employ them, run them into the ground."

Reed didn't comment. He knew where this was headed and didn't feel like playing along. Oliver Enfield was a monster of a man, but so was Gambit.

Gambit tilted his head to one side. "Enfield had a deal with you, right? He usually did that. A certain number of kills in exchange for some big favor. Freedom, in your case."

"Thirty kills," Reed said.

"Ah, thirty kills. How many had you completed when, you know . . . you backed out?"

"Twenty-nine."

Gambit appeared shocked, but Reed doubted it was genuine. He probably knew all of this already and was just fishing for something else.

"You gave up so close to the end. Wouldn't it have been easier to . . . *finish the job*?"

Reed smirked. "When the Holiday hit was ordered—by *your boss*—Oliver knew it was my last job. He knew I planned to quit afterward, so he set me up. He was planning for the FBI to bust me and cart me back to prison. But you already knew that. I bet you know all about me, which is why you went to the trouble of getting me here—to leave me in the dark, chained to a table."

Gambit returned the smirk. "I like to hear things from the horse's mouth."

Reed didn't respond. He stared Gambit down, waiting for the man to break under the silence. It didn't take long.

"Here's the thing, Reed. Like I told you in the woods, I have a job for you. A delicate job. A job that really . . . *really* needs to be done."

"And you're wondering if I'm going to *back out*."

Gambit shook his head. "No, I know you won't. Unlike Enfield, I understand that the best way to motivate a man is to believe in him. If you help him get the thing he wants, he'll help you get the thing you want. And Reed, I have the thing you want."

Some of the boiling anger that bubbled just beneath the surface spilled through Reed's forced calm. His lips twisted into a sneer, and his next words came out as a growl.

"Well, let me out of these cuffs, and let's get to it."

Gambit cocked his head, regarding Reed with the appraising eye of a man selecting a steak at the grocery store. Probing. Thoughtful. Unsure.

He shook his head. "I don't think so, Reed. I'm not certain you're committed yet. I'm just not feeling it."

Gambit turned toward the door, and Reed sat up, clenching his teeth. "Where's my father?"

The door swung open, and this time, blinding light poured in. Reed sat back and shielded his face.

"Your father is safe, Reed. Maybe, when I'm feeling your commitment, you can see him. But don't worry, there's no rush. *I can do this for days.*"

Gambit disappeared into the light, and the door smacked shut.

3

The first thing Banks recognized was the ceiling fan. It spun slowly over her face, its blades drooping from a dirty brass fixture. She blinked, but the picture didn't clarify. It was still blurry, and a further blink made her eyes sting.

Everything hurt. Her back, limbs, and abs were sore from days of jumping, running, and dodging bullets, but her face hurt the most. It felt swollen and pressurized, as though her brain were trapped inside a helium balloon.

What the hell happened to me? Where am I?

Nothing about the small bedroom was in any way familiar. Nobody else was in the room—at least that she could see. In fact, the only thing her disoriented mind could process was the ceiling fan. It squeaked every two seconds, just audibly enough to be heard through the blur. Had the squeak woken her? Maybe it was the pain.

The throbbing in her face began to clarify. The epicenter of the pain was her nose, and from there, blasts of agony shot outward. There was a headache, too.

Banks lifted her right hand and fished for her nose. It was difficult for some reason, as if she couldn't find it. Her fingers touched something soft, but it wasn't her nose. It was tissue paper jammed *into* her nose. And then, an inch or so higher . . .

Banks jerked her hand back and grimaced. Her head exploded in pain, and tears spilled down her cheeks.

What the hell happened to me?

She focused on the fan, blocking out the pain while she tried to recall her most recent memory. *Where was I?*

Wyoming. The memory of driving back from Wyoming with Reed was pretty clear. They were in a stolen car, and there was an incident with some assassins in Kansas. *Is that where the pain came from?*

No, she survived that event. *What happened next?*

The memories flooded back now, piled one on top of the other. They made it to Mississippi and met the funny Mexican with the panel van full of weapons. Reed bought some things, and then they drove to Alabama—she couldn't remember where exactly—and rented a hotel for the rest of the day. Reed wanted to move at night to the prison . . . the prison where his father was housed.

So they waited until the sun faded, then Reed drove down a long, rural road a couple miles from the prison. Nobody else was there. He parked the car, gathered his things . . .

Did he leave her there? She thought so. She thought she remembered waiting in the car, then getting out because she heard something. Voices, or sirens, or something. She was outside the car, looking for Reed . . . then, nothing.

Her nose erupted in another surge of pain so sudden she wanted to puke, but she couldn't even swallow.

Whatever happened next, it most definitely involved her nose colliding with something.

The phone. The thought rang through her tired mind like a bullet. She blinked and pawed at the blankets and in her pockets, searching for the little plastic device. It was nowhere to be found.

Her heart began to thump a little harder. *Is Reed here? Did he make it out of the prison okay? Is he okay? Where is the damn phone?*

A foot tapped against the floor outside the bedroom. Banks froze, suddenly very aware that she was alone and unarmed. What if Reed wasn't here? Who brought her to this place?

The door opened and then groaned against old hinges. Another footfall sounded against the floor, light and gentle, as though it were the step of a child. Banks blinked rapidly, trying to clear her vision.

She twisted her head to the left, and a moment later, a figure stepped close to the bed.

It wasn't a child, although the woman standing next to Banks wasn't much bigger than one. She was only a foot away, her petite body leaned over the bed. Smooth red hair was swept over one shoulder, and bright green eyes shone down.

The woman had a nice face and a gentle smile. Soft fingers touched Banks's arm and then traced their way toward her face.

Banks pulled away.

"Hey now." The voice was warm, with no dominant accent. "You're awake."

"Who are you?" Banks croaked. They were her first words in god only knew how long, and they rasped against a dry throat.

The woman's smile widened, and she produced a glass of water with a straw from next to the bed.

"I'm Lucy," she said. "We met in Alabama yesterday."

Banks gulped down the water as if it were the last drink on the planet and was disappointed to hear the empty rattle of bubbles shooting up the straw only moments later.

Lucy took the glass away and stroked Banks's hand.

"Actually, I don't know your name. I couldn't find your ID."

Banks licked her lips, still desperate for another drink. *Why is this woman here? Is she a friend of Reed's or a friend of the other people?*

Banks decided there wasn't much risk in sharing her name—her first name, anyway. Lucy had done as much.

"I'm Banks," she said.

Lucy nodded once, her attention now directed at Banks's swollen nose.

"That's a lovely name," she said. "Can't say that I've heard it before, but I like it."

"Was . . . was there anybody with me?" Banks asked. She didn't want to volunteer any information, but she had to know.

Lucy looked away, back to the nightstand, and fiddled with a bag. She produced medical supplies and began to remove the tissue paper crammed into Banks's nose.

"You mean Reed," Lucy said.

Banks winced, both at the pain of her nose being prodded and the mention of his name. A sudden swelling erupted in her throat, and she blinked a couple times.

"You know him?"

"Oh, yes," Lucy said. She wiped Banks's face with a damp cloth. "I've known Reed for a while now."

Something about her words, the gentle way she said them, and that little tagline *a while now*, ignited a strange irritation in Banks. She wasn't sure why, but she suddenly felt jealous. She wanted to smack Lucy right across her pretty china-doll face.

Lucy met her gaze and blushed. "Oh, no, sweetheart. Not like that. Reed and I are, well, we *were* business associates. We worked for the same firm."

"Wait, don't tell me. You're a venture capitalist." Banks's voice dripped with sarcasm.

Lucy laughed. "No, sweetie. I kill people for a living."

Her words were so frank that there wasn't anything left to say. Banks lay quietly while Lucy finished swabbing and replacing the tissue paper with fresh gauze.

"I'm very sorry about your nose," she said. There was a question in her tone, but Banks ignored it.

"Was Reed there?" Banks asked.

Lucy looked back into her bag and offered a small smile. "No, I didn't see Reed. Although, based on news reports, I have a pretty good idea where he was. He's spending a lot of time on the news these days, isn't he?"

Another loaded question that Banks chose to ignore. She felt something stinging the edges of her vision, and she tried to sit up.

Lucy placed a hand on her shoulder and pressed her back into the sheets.

"Lie down, now. I'm going to give you a little something to help you sleep."

Before Banks could stop her, she felt a sharp sting in the crook of her elbow. The sting was gone as soon as it came, and Banks fell back against the pillow as Lucy continued to stroke her arm and speak in soft sentences.

Lucy's words began to fade, as did the pounding headache. The last thing Banks remembered was the rhythmic squeak of the fan.

―――――

Lucy watched Banks sink into the sheets, her eyelids growing heavy as her attention faded. It was a beautiful face full of warmth. At least it had been before it was smashed into the roof of the rusty old sedan Lucy found parked two miles from the prison.

She had a pretty good idea who had done the smashing. The slender footprints that surrounded the car were too small to be Banks's or Reed's, but that evidence was superfluous.

Lucy replaced the syringe in her pack. Banks would sleep eight or ten hours on that dose, and she desperately needed it. Lucy had reset her broken nose the night before, but the cartilage was busted, bruised, and inflamed. It would take weeks to heal and would remain sensitive the entire time.

What a bitch move, she thought, busting another woman's face like that.

Lucy left the room, locking the door behind her. She wasn't holding Banks hostage, but she wanted to be sure her patient didn't wander into the woods. Holly Springs was a massive forest, and it would be easy to get lost.

Outside the bedroom, the remainder of the cabin consisted of a small bathroom and a kitchen-living room combination, complete with a stone fireplace. It was a hunting cabin built on private land inside the national forest. She liked to rent it on occasion, usually for vacation, but this was the first time she'd used it as a safe house.

Lucy stepped outside the cabin, her tiny shoes squeaking in the mud as she walked around back to the entrance of the storm cellar. She swung one of the twin doors open, then flipped the light on as she slipped down the stairs.

A third woman waited at the bottom, tied to a chair, her mouth gagged. She wasn't big by any stretch, but looked like a giant next to Lucy. Raven hair covered her head and hung down over a twisted, mutilated face. Burn marks crisscrossed the woman's entire body, disappearing beneath her shirt. Lucy had traced each of them when she gently bathed the woman after knocking her out cold in the woods and before tying her to this chair.

Lucy might have been a killer, but she wasn't a monster. She was a warrior, and the warrior respected her defeated foe.

She stepped forward, and the woman's eyes darted toward her, sending venomous waves of anger across the storm cellar. Lucy gave her a pitiable smile and took another step, then gently tugged the gag out of the woman's mouth.

"Now then," Lucy said. "It's time we had a little chat."

4

Governor Maggie Trousdale collapsed over her desk, her face in her hands, and sobbed. The darkened office around her was silent and empty, the dull city lights blocked out by blinds.

Governor for mere months, and now this, an erupting scandal that threatened to undermine everything she had ever worked for. When Maggie ran for office, it was because she believed in something, and when she won, it was because the people believed in it, too. There was corruption in Louisiana. Corruption from the seashore to the Mighty Mississippi, from the forests of upstate to the plains at the Texas state line. And the epicenter of it all was Baton Rouge, a city inundated by decades of dirty politics and dirtier money.

Maggie was going to change that. She would rip it out by the roots and run a campaign based on integrity, not money and self-interest.

The door to her office clicked, and Attorney General Robert Coulier, her personal appointment after the assassination of Attorney General Matthews a few weeks prior, stepped inside. He was a shrewd man, verging on ruthless, which was part of why she hired him. Certainly, it wasn't because of his outstanding legal record, which was, in fact, stained with numerous controversies and disbarment in the state of Texas, but because he was relentless and dedicated. She called him her *pit bull*, the man who was going to help her destroy corruption.

So much for that.

Coulier settled into a wingback chair in front of her desk. His face was cold, his eyes unblinking behind round glasses.

What a comfort.

"Madam Governor, you have to decide."

Maggie looked away. She swallowed back the lump in her throat and ignored the wet trails on her face. She didn't care if Coulier saw her this way. He knew the corner she was in.

"I can't do it," she said. "Dan is innocent. You know that."

Coulier grunted. Daniel Sharp was Maggie's lieutenant governor, a man who had campaigned beside her under the same banner of integrity-based leadership. LGs were independently elected in Louisiana, but it was no secret that Sharp was only interested in the job if Maggie was elected. No secret that he was only running because she asked him to.

She closed her eyes. Why had she asked Sharp to run? Because of his sincerity. His wise counsel. Sharp was an emotional man, but he always spoke the truth. She picked him because he could keep her focused, and he had until she'd decided to cut him out of the loop and pursue a dangerous path of self-destruction she knew he would never endorse.

There was some manner of illegal operation happening at the Port of New Orleans. Maggie wasn't sure what, but she had brushed up with the man running it—a man who called himself Gambit—and he had threatened her family, which made the fight personal. It was Coulier's idea to pin Gambit down by closing the port—an idea that Sharp had vehemently opposed. But Maggie was ready for bold action, and Coulier said he had a safe and legal way to close the port.

Well, he never said safe *or* legal. Maggie inferred those virtues on his reckless plan. Coulier slipped some heavy metal toxins into the harbor under the noses of a research team from LSU. When the toxins were discovered, Maggie responded by declaring a state of emergency and closing the port.

The idea was to flush Gambit out by applying pressure to his operations. It didn't work, and now the entire scheme was in danger of being exposed.

"Madam Governor, you have to let me protect you." Coulier's voice was dry and monotone. "Nobody could've predicted this outcome, but it happened. Now we have to manage the fallout."

Maggie shook her head. "I'm going to resign and come clean. Dan will become governor to finish out my term."

"And then what?" Coulier leaned forward. "Do you really think he has what it takes to fulfill your mandate? Dan is a good man, but what Louisiana needs is a strong leader, somebody willing to get their hands dirty. What did your supporters call you? *Muddy Maggie?*"

"They called me that because I'm from the swamps. Because I'm one of them."

"So *be* one of them. Get down in the mud. Get the job done."

Maggie turned toward the window. She couldn't see through the blinds at the crowds of reporters gathered at the steps of the Capitol outside, but she knew they were there. The reporters, protestors, unemployed dock workers, and port officers were there because of *her*. Because of what *she* did.

"Maggie."

She stiffened. Coulier never called her by her first name. Even now, there was no familiarity in his tone—only strength and command.

"You are about to jeopardize the future, security, and integrity of this state," he said. "People *you* promised to protect. Don't be a coward. Do what a weak leader could never do, and allow me to protect the integrity of this administration."

Maggie met his gaze for a long moment, then looked down and nodded.

Coulier stood up, leaned across the desk, and placed a file in front of her. It was an official statement typed on her own letterhead, and she signed without reading it. She already knew it was a memo from the governor's office condemning the illegal conspiracy of the lieutenant governor.

"Once the smoke clears and we've run these bastards to ground, you will issue Sharp an executive pardon. He'll never serve a day for poisoning the harbor or for any related activities. After all, he had the best intentions. Your victory over the corruption in this state will prove that."

Maggie nodded again, but she didn't look up.

"There's one final thing. I hate to ask, but it's necessary. You have to confront Dan. Make sure he'll be a team player."

Maggie's gaze snapped up as footsteps rang out in the hallway, and she shook her head, but it was too late. Coulier stepped back, and the door opened.

Lieutenant Governor Daniel Sharp rushed into the room. His tie swung loosely around his neck, and dark bags hung beneath his eyes. He rushed to the desk and pulled Maggie into a hug before she could stop him.

"My god, Maggie. I've been looking for you all day. Are you all right?"

He peered down at her, his face flooded with concern.

She began to cry, not even trying to hold it back.

"Maggie, we'll get through this," Sharp said. "Whatever it takes, I'll never leave your side. The executive branch will hold together."

Maggie took a step back, and confusion crossed Sharp's face as she broke free of his hands and shook her head.

As though on cue, his gaze drifted down to the signed statement on her desk.

"Maggie . . ."

He scanned the page, then scooped it up and read it in full. His hands shook. "Maggie, what the hell?"

Boots rang out in the hallway, running toward her office, and the three of them looked to the door as half a dozen men in black suits burst in.

The lead man made directly for Sharp, stepping around the desk and producing a badge from beneath his coat.

"Mr. Lieutenant Governor, Agent Don Kritz, Louisiana Bureau of Investigation. You're under arrest."

Four other men stood back, their hands on their weapons, while a fifth stepped forward and helped Agent Kritz bend Sharp over the desk. Before anyone could speak, Kritz was reading Sharp his rights and hauling him toward the door.

"Wait!" Maggie screamed, and she rushed forward, blocking the way. "What are you doing?"

"Madam Governor, step aside."

"Where are you taking him?"

"Into custody. Please step aside."

She held up her hand. "Agent, I'm your governor! Charges of conspiracy do not warrant an arrest of this violence."

"Conspiracy?" Kritz twisted his head. "Madam Governor, LG Sharp is under arrest for murder."

"Murder?" She felt the blood drain from her face. "*Who?*"

"Attorney General Matthews, ma'am. I can't comment further. Step aside."

The six men were gone as quickly as they came, rushing out of the office and allowing the doors to clap shut behind them.

Maggie's head spun. She stumbled back and felt Coulier catch her by the elbow.

"Coulier, my god. What have you done?"

"Nothing, I swear. The evidence was only supposed to implicate him in the conspiracy of poisoning the port."

He helped Maggie into a chair.

She collapsed as the tears continued to flow. "My god . . . my god."

Coulier gritted his teeth. "We'll get to the bottom of this. It has to be a mix-up."

She sobbed. "I can't pardon him for this. I can't touch this!"

The room fell silent, and Coulier placed a gentle hand on her shoulder. "I know. And you won't have to. It's just you and me now."

5

The Mercedes purred to a stop, its sleek outline little more than a shadow on the dark forest road. The headlights were off, and the brake lights had been disconnected using an aftermarket switch mounted beneath the dash. From behind the tinted glass, it was difficult to make out more than the vague shapes of tree trunks, but Wolfgang knew where he was going.

He shifted into park, then cut the engine. Other than the gentle ticking of the cooling motor, the forest road lay silent as a graveyard.

He chewed softly on a wad of gum, surveying the darkened trees for five minutes before redirecting his attention to the handheld computer in the passenger's seat. The screen was backlit in red, protecting his natural night vision as he manipulated it with two fingers. On the computer screen, the vague mark of the cell phone signal still blinked at a location three hundred yards north of the main road. A dirt track led in that direction, with fresh tire marks in the mud.

Wolfgang rubbed his chin, his gaze switching between the computer and the dirt track, then he pocketed the device and stepped out of the car.

The night air was chilly but a lot warmer than the snow-filled wind he left in New York State the previous day. He buttoned his peacoat, then proceeded to the rear of the car.

The red trunk light glowed softly as he retrieved his combat belt and strapped it on over the peacoat. Two large handguns—Glock semi-automatics chambered in 10mm—were strapped on either side of the belt, with a flashlight, a knife, and a choke cord joining them. The choke cord and knife were designated for primary use, while the handguns were reserved for a worst-case scenario. He carried 10mm because it was a faultlessly reliable round, almost always delivering a kill on the first shot. Many years before, he had almost lost his life when a small-caliber handgun failed to drop his assailant after multiple shots, and that was a mistake he would never make again.

After securing the belt over his hips, he checked both guns to ensure they were chambered and ready to fire, then started into the woods, keeping the dirt track parallel to his own course about ten yards to the left. He didn't expect any sort of electronic surveillance, but walking directly on the track would leave him far too exposed.

The moon overhung the forest, half-full, filling the spaces between the trees with silver light. On any other night, Wolfgang might have paused to appreciate the natural beauty of the forest or to wait quietly in the dark, hoping for a chance to see some kind of nocturnal animal make a star-lit appearance. He enjoyed a lot of nights like that by himself in the woods of Upstate New York—probably more than was healthy, considering his astounding lack of a social life.

Occupational hazards, he guessed. Professional assassins weren't known for their thriving circle of friends. Not the ones who enjoyed long careers, anyway.

Deeper into the forest, his own footfalls rang louder in his ears. Each crunch of a leaf or snap of a twig sounded like a gunshot, and he slowed his pace even further. It wasn't far to the cabin now. He hadn't checked the computer in over three hundred yards, but he knew he was close. Another bend in the track, up a little hill, and there it was.

The cabin sat alone with darkened windows and no hint of occupancy other than the dingy sedan parked next to the door. It was a hideous thing —some kind of Buick or Mercury. Wolfgang recognized Kansas license plates on the car and wondered for a moment if Reed had really driven that rattletrap all the way back from the Sunflower State.

If he had, it could mean Reed was avoiding attention, driving something forgettable. Or it could mean that his resources were dwindling, and rapidly so.

It didn't matter. Wolfgang would find out soon enough. He retrieved a pistol from his belt and started toward the cabin. His footfalls were silent, as carefully placed as the paws of a lynx slipping up to the cabin without so much as the whisper of grass being bent in the wind. With each step, he monitored the cabin for any signs of life—a creak from the floorboards, a glint in the window.

There was nothing. Were it not for the car, the cabin would've looked abandoned, and that itself was a reflection of Reed's peculiar talents as an assassin. Homes were living organisms that reacted in strange ways to the presence or absence of occupants. It wasn't just the lack of light or sound— an empty home *felt* empty when you looked at it. Reed knew how to make a home feel that way even when he was inside.

Well, Wolfgang knew a few tricks of his own, like how to make a home feel on fire.

He skipped the steps, which appeared creaky, and opted to mount the porch by rolling onto its far edge. There was no railing, and it took only a moment to regain his footing and approach the entrance. An old, torn screen door would also likely give away his presence, but a quick application of WD-40 from a small can in his pocket ensured that wouldn't be an issue.

The main door would certainly be locked. He could kick it open and breach the house, which would alert Reed, but since the cabin was a small single-story, he probably wouldn't have time to react. Alternatively, Wolfgang could pick the lock . . .

The door wasn't locked. The knob twisted in perfect silence, and the door swung open without a sound. Wolfgang braced his tense muscles and raised the gun as he stepped across the threshold and into darkness.

He cleared the door, braced his shooting hand with his left hand, and started toward the kitchen.

From his left, something bright and silver flashed across his face, and a split second later, he was critically aware of that same glimmering item a millimeter from his neck, hovering in absolute stillness.

It was a razor-sharp blade only a breath away from severing his windpipe.

"One more step, and you'll be catching your head with your hands."

The female's voice was perfectly calm but loaded to the brim with menace.

Wolfgang swallowed, then lowered the gun and offered a tight smirk without turning his head.

"Nasty greeting. I heard Mississippians were hospitable."

"You heard wrong," the voice said, its speaker still shrouded in darkness. "A Mississippian would've shot you already. It's lucky I'm not one. Now, drop the gun and the belt."

Wolfgang rotated the handgun onto its side and dropped it onto the rug. It fell with a thud, followed a moment later by the belt.

"I'd usually buy you dinner before dropping my belt." Wolfgang's smirk widened.

"Don't flatter yourself, honey. The bigger the gun, the smaller the gun . . . if you know what I mean."

Wolfgang could feel the blood rushing to his cheeks as the blade twitched beneath his chin.

"Move to the table, and sit down in the nearest chair. Remember, I'm a hell of a lot faster with this blade than you are with your lame pickup lines."

Wolfgang stepped slowly toward the table, sliding a wooden chair back from the end and settling into it.

The woman followed, pivoting in front of him and keeping the tip of the blade less than an inch from his throat the entire time. He could see the weapon now. It was a sword of some type—single-edged and gently curved. Japanese, maybe. But he still couldn't see her face.

Wolfgang held up both hands. "All right. You've got me in the chair. How much for a dance?"

The blade twitched with the speed of a bullet, flicking across his face and clipping the end of his nose. He didn't feel the cut, but a moment later, large drops of blood began dripping into his lap. He recoiled as the sword hovered only millimeters from his nose.

"I'd chill with the smack if I were you."

Wolfgang didn't move, his gaze riveted on the tip of the weapon. Who *was* this person? The woman he saw with Reed back in North Carolina and Tennessee? Couldn't be. If Reed were here, he would've already barreled through the room like a charging bull, cursing and blowing things up.

Maybe this woman was holding him prisoner. None of the possibilities were favorable.

"Banks, honey!" The woman's voice rose in a gentle shout. "If you're awake, I could really use your help."

There was a pause, and then the woman called again for Banks—whoever that was.

A hallway floorboard creaked, followed by the thump of sleepy feet. A light flashed on, and Wolfgang blinked, his eyes flooded by the flash of white. As he struggled to regain his vision, he heard another couple footfalls and then the thunk of somebody stopping with a jolt.

"*You!*"

Wolfgang's vision returned. He could see his captor now: a petite woman, no more than five feet tall, with scarlet hair and stunning green eyes. She held the sword with one steady hand while the other hand was pinned against her hips.

But it wasn't the redhead who had exclaimed. Behind her, standing at the end of the hallway, was a taller woman with blonde hair, sleepy blue eyes, and a nose so swollen and red it looked like some kind of rotten vegetable. It was the woman from North Carolina. The woman with Reed.

Her eyes blazed with hatred, and she started forward, raising a fist.

Wolfgang recoiled and held up both hands. "Hey! Listen! Before things get out of hand, I feel like I should clarify. I wasn't trying to kill you in Carolina. I mean, it was kind of a mis—"

"Oh, so you were lobbing grenades at me to make me *feel good* about myself?" Her voice cracked with emotion.

Wolfgang grimaced. "Okay, see, when you say it like that, it makes me sound all kinds of violent. Let's get some coffee and—"

"Shut up," the redhead said. She flicked the sword again, just beneath his eyeline, and he froze. "Banks, honey, look in the kitchen. There's got to be some tape around here."

Banks glared at Wolfgang, but she stumbled into the kitchen and began rifling through drawers. She reappeared moments later with a roll of duct tape and followed the redhead's directions in securing Wolfgang hand and foot to the chair. With every pass of the tape, Banks glared daggers at him.

Wolfgang redirected his attention to the woman with the sword. There was something very peculiar going on. Reed obviously wasn't around, but if the blonde woman was, then the redhead knew about Reed. Who was she anyway? Not another girlfriend, surely. Was Reed like that?

Banks stepped back from her handiwork and folded her arms.

The redhead pivoted in front of the chair and laid the flat of the blade against Wolfgang's shoulder, its edge only a millimeter from his neck.

"Banks, you know this man?"

Banks nodded, her bottom lip poked out in a mild pout.

Matched with her brutalized nose, Wolfgang couldn't imagine a more pitiful face.

"He's some kind of assassin. I don't know his name."

"Wolfgang," he said with a tired sigh. "Wolfgang Pierce. And seriously, you've got it all wrong."

The redhead raised an eyebrow. "Is that right? Well, why don't you enlighten us, *Mr. Pierce*? Why are you here?"

Wolfgang assumed his most innocent smile. "Because Reed sent for me."

6

Gambit stood outside Montgomery's prison cell and drew a long breath. Stress radiated from his body, leaving his muscles feeling like violin strings that were stretched too tight, played too hard. The last few days had been a whirlwind of events, most of which had spun completely out of his control. Being out of control was an alarming sensation, and one he wasn't accustomed to. Gambit prided himself on never losing control and always being on top. It was his greatest virtue and what made him so valuable to Aiden.

It was what kept him alive.

Gambit stepped away from the door and paced for a moment. Montgomery could never feel his stress or know how weak Gambit's bargaining position actually was. If he did, the big killer would almost certainly take control.

Gambit could play coy with Montgomery and make little comments like "I can do this for days" all he wanted, but in the end, he was little more than a paper tiger. He couldn't afford to waste any time in deploying Montgomery against Governor Trousdale. Things were moving quickly in Louisiana, and what began as a snag was starting to appear like a potential exposure. The LBI had just arrested Lieutenant Governor Sharp in conjunction with the Attorney General Matthews killing, which would've been good news if Gambit were trying to pin that death on somebody.

The problem was, he hadn't been. Gambit paid what he believed to be a top-notch assassin to knock off Matthews—a ruthless prosecutor who was becoming increasingly dangerous to Aiden's operation in Louisiana. The assassin claimed to be a specialist in natural death appearances, but as it turned out, he probably wasn't a specialist in wiping his own ass. The toxicologists easily detected the poison in Matthews's blood, which triggered an investigation that Gambit never intended to deal with. The situation had become a virtual time bomb, threatening to sink Aiden's operation at any moment.

Matthews was now more of a loose end than Trousdale was, which was why it was so critical to send Montgomery to finish the job. Aiden didn't know how bad things were with the Matthews investigation. If things went well with Montgomery, he would never know. Montgomery would cap Trousdale, Gambit would ensure that he was caught for it, and then Gambit would drop a few extra bread crumbs that led investigators to charge Montgomery with the death of AG Matthews also.

It was perfect, really. A disgraced former Marine who escaped from prison going on a slaughter spree against state-level politicians. First, a state senator from Georgia, then an attorney general from Louisiana, and finally, the governor of Louisiana herself. All of Aiden's problems cleaned up, pinned on a likely suspect, and swept away into a story the media would gobble down like candy.

Gambit gnawed on his fingernails. The only problem was Montgomery, of course. He had already proven himself to be a formidable foe, both clever and efficient. Sure, Gambit never expected Oliver Enfield's arsenal of killers to be able to knock off The Prosecutor, but he was still surprised by how absolutely ineffective they were. Montgomery was a man of prowess, with zero hesitation guarding his trigger finger. Gambit had a tiger by the tail, and he wasn't quite ready to let go.

But he couldn't wait much longer, either. With Lieutenant Governor Sharp behind bars, screaming to his lawyers and arguing with investigators, it was only a matter of time before he was found guiltless, which would redirect heat back to the case, and possibly back to Gambit.

Why the hell had the LBI arrested Sharp, anyway?

Gambit stopped at the end of the hall and pulled at his lip. He had to focus and narrow his mind down to the problem at hand. Sharp, the LBI, and all the rest could wait. Right now, he had to decide about Montgomery. He could let him off the leash now, smack his ass, and tell him to run down Trousdale. And Montgomery might do it.

Or he might attempt to double-cross Gambit and rescue David. That was the problem with holding something over Montgomery's head—he might bite your arm off. That was what happened to Oliver Enfield, certainly, and it was why Gambit tried to present himself as the prophet of hope instead of the god of damnation.

He wasn't sure it was working. Montgomery was such a hard man to read. In the forest outside the prison, Gambit knew he was getting to Reed; it was blatantly obvious. But now, a couple days after Montgomery had time to sit and think, had he regained control of himself?

That was another problem with further delays. It gave Montgomery more time to *think*. More time to calculate a way out of this.

Gambit tasted blood and realized he'd split one of his fingernails. He winced and wrung his hand, sending a splatter of crimson across the floor.

Think, dammit. He had to think. If he acted now, it might be too soon. But if he waited, so much more could go wrong.

Gambit crammed his hand into his pocket, cursing his mind into silence. He couldn't allow the panic to take over. His very life was on the line here, and if he wanted to survive, he had to regain control.

He ran one hand through his hair, then straightened his tie. He always wore a suit because it made him feel in charge—professional and prepared. It was time to be the boss. Time to take control.

Without another thought, he stomped back down the hallway and inserted his key into the lock. Light spilled over his shoulders and into the dark room, exposing Montgomery sitting just as he had when Gambit last saw him eight hours prior—chained to the table, staring forward.

Montgomery was impassive. As resilient as a stone wall.

Gambit pushed inside the door and forced a smile. The tension and doubt he felt was concealed beneath a shroud of practiced confidence—his own version of a stone wall.

"Feeling fresh, Reed?"

Montgomery blinked but didn't say anything.

"I have good news for you," Gambit said. "I've thought of a way you can prove yourself to me. Prove that you're ready for your primary mission."

Montgomery raised an eyebrow but still didn't speak.

Gambit wanted to beat him in the face with a pipe wrench, but he remained calm.

Focus on the objective, he reminded himself. Get what you want. Get what you deserve.

"I know you're a man of conscience," Gambit continued. "A man who makes his own judgments about morality, and that's what concerns me. I'm concerned that you'll second-guess my judgments. Maybe, when the moment is close, and it's time to pull the trigger, you'll think you know better than I do."

Montgomery grunted. It was all at once a condescending and indifferent sound that made Gambit's blood boil, but still, he remained calm.

"It's a problem, Reed, but I've thought of a way we can test your resolve. Your ability to trust my judgment. Are you interested?"

"Only if it gets me out of this room and closer to my father."

Montgomery's voice was cold, but Gambit could hear concealed pain. That was good. It meant that Montgomery was thinking about his father, pining after the hope that David wasn't completely mad . . . that he could be saved.

What a fool.

"I'm a man of my word, Reed. You'll get your father back. But first, you have to prove your loyalty."

"I'm listening."

"There's a federal judge in Little Rock, Arkansas, by the name of Sheila Perry. She's fifty-eight years old, has a husband, two kids, and four grandchildren. She's enjoyed a flawless, decorated career, gives generously to charity, and is adored by her friends and community. She's never broken a rule, Reed. The woman doesn't even have a parking ticket. She gets to work before the sun rises and leaves after it sets. She is, by every traditional, moral measuring stick, a *good woman*."

Montgomery's face remained impassive, but Gambit thought he could see a spark deep in his eyes. A hint of understanding.

Gambit smiled. "So, what I want, Reed . . . what you can do to prove that you trust my judgment and will do whatever I say, is drive to Arkansas, ambush her in her office, and break her neck."

7

"What do you mean *he sent for you?*" Lucy's voice dripped with sarcasm as she held the blade against her prisoner's shoulder, though it wasn't necessary. Banks had wrapped him in enough tape to subdue a lion, but she liked the way his attention fixated on the sword with the nervous energy of a convict eying the executioner's ax.

It was kind of sexy.

Wolfgang waggled his fingers, about the only part of his limbs that could move. "Well, when I said he sent for me, I meant that somebody sent for me on his behalf . . . I think. There was a notecard. It's all a little complicated. Can I speak to him, please?"

Banks stood next to Lucy with her arms crossed. Lucy didn't know her well enough to determine what emotion she was feeling, but Banks was far from calm—that much was obvious. She stared the prisoner down in stony silence, waiting for Lucy to make the next move.

"Who sent for you?" Lucy asked.

Wolfgang shrugged. "Like I said, it's complicated. I came here to discuss it with him. I really—"

"He's lying," Banks said. "He tried to kill us both!"

"Both?" Lucy said.

"Me and Reed. We were in the mountains in North Carolina. He showed up with some kind of shotgun thing that fired grenades and tried to blow us away. *He ran my car off the road!*"

Lucy stared down the length of the sword. "Is that true?"

Wolfgang held up a finger. "I didn't run any cars off the road. Reed did that because he's a sucky driver. He wrecks cars. It's kind of his signature."

Banks lunged forward and smacked Wolfgang across the face. The movement was so sudden and savage that Lucy didn't have time to react. The sound of flesh on flesh cracked through the cabin like a gunshot, and Wolfgang's head snapped back.

Banks growled, "Listen, you bastard. He's twice the driver you'll ever be. *Why are you here?*"

Wolfgang spit blood from his lips. "I *told you*. I need to talk to Reed. Man, you're one crazy—"

Another smack, then a third. Each time, Wolfgang's head bounced back as though he'd been hit with a baseball bat.

"Crazy *what*?" Banks screamed. "What kind of crazy am I?"

Lucy slid the sword back into its scabbard and stood back, her arms folded.

Two more lightning smacks cracked against Wolfgang's face, then Banks held out her hand.

"Lucy, give me something sharp."

Lucy put one hand on her shoulder.

"Banks, honey, I think he's had enough. We'll get the truth, don't worry."

Banks glowered at Lucy but reluctantly stepped away from Wolfgang. Their prisoner sat up, blinking back tears and spitting out blood.

"Who *are you*?" he snapped.

Banks growled, "I'm a Mississippi redneck, bitch, and you're getting on my nerves."

"Clearly. . . ." He shook his head as if to clear it, then spat out more blood.

"I think you should get him a towel," Lucy said. "We don't want him choking."

Banks snorted but didn't move. Lucy shot her a sideways glare, and with another sigh, Banks retreated to the kitchen.

Lucy turned back to Wolfgang.

"I don't think either one of us wants an encore of that performance. You better start again, with the truth."

Banks returned with the towel and roughly swabbed Wolfgang's mouth. He swallowed once, spit again, then leaned back in the chair.

"Start talking," Lucy said.

Wolfgang glowered. "Okay, but she better stay back."

"Or *what*?" Banks snapped.

Lucy held up a hand. "Calm down, Banks. He's going to cooperate now."

They looked down at Wolfgang, and Lucy tapped her foot.

"All right. The truth. I was hired to hunt and kill Reed by a man named Salvador. He originally hired Oliver Enfield to use Reed to kill Senator Mitchell Holiday, but when that all blew up, Salvador needed to tie up loose ends, and Reed was one of them. So, he sent me to North Carolina to kill Reed."

"That's where the grenades came in?" Lucy asked.

"Yes. I made a couple passes at Montgomery but couldn't seal the deal. I had a third shot at him in Cherokee, a little town—"

"I know where it is," Lucy said.

"Right. So, I almost had him, but at the last moment, Salvador called me off. Apparently, Oliver's people were at Holiday's cabin by the lake, and they were going to finish the job. So I disengaged."

Wolfgang swallowed blood again, and Lucy made a "get on with it" motion with her hand.

"Reed made a mess by the lake. I'm fuzzy on the details, but apparently, he massacred Oliver's crew. Salvador called me again to finish the job, which I was going to do, but I had to go to Scotland first to graduate."

"To *graduate*?" Banks said. "Ha! What, were you passing the GED?"

Wolfgang smirked. "Actually, I completed a doctorate in medical science."

Lucy shot Banks a sideways look.

"Anyway. I was in Scotland, and Salvador kept hounding me. I planned to finish the job, but I guess Reed put too much pressure on Salvador, because by the time I made it back to the states . . ."

Wolfgang hesitated, and his eyes turned cold.

"Let's hear it," Lucy snapped.

"Salvador decided I required additional motivation. He kidnapped somebody important to me and held them as ransom in exchange for Reed's life."

Banks crossed her arms and stuck her chin out. "Mm-hmm. And how did that make you *feel*?"

Wolfgang gave her a milk-curdling glare. "Don't patronize me. I kill people for a living, but that doesn't mean there aren't people I care about, and I also have rules. One of them is that my personal life is left alone. Salvador broke that rule, so I tracked him down in Nashville and found him in the middle of a gunfight with Reed. There was another car wreck, of course."

Lucy turned a questioning glance toward Banks, and she nodded. It was true.

"What then?" Lucy asked.

Wolfgang's stare was cold and absolute. "I took care of my business."

Lucy saw a block wall in his eyes, and she decided it was time to redirect to present circumstances.

"Why are you here? Did somebody else pay you to kill Reed?"

Wolfgang leaned back in the chair. "No. I told you the truth. Somebody sent me a card claiming that Reed has something. Something I need. I'm here to talk to him about it."

"What *something*?" Banks asked.

Wolfgang's glare was defiant. "I'm not discussing that."

"Is that right?" Banks started forward again, but Lucy held her back.

"Calm down, honey. We'll get to it."

She turned back to Wolfgang. "Why should we believe you?"

"Because I'm telling the truth."

Lucy smirked. "According to you."

The razor wit had faded from Wolfgang's expression. "Listen to me. Your friend Montgomery is mixed up in something really, really serious. I don't know the details, and I don't know what your angle is, but believe me when I tell you it's about to get much worse. I'm willing to help him get out of it in exchange for what he has. It's worth that much to me."

"So you don't want to kill him?" Lucy asked.

"I don't."

"Then why did you sneak in here last night, gun drawn?"

"I'm a tactically wary person."

"Fair enough. How did you find us?"

"Two days ago, Reed bought a pair of burner phones off an arms dealer they call T-Rex. I tracked one of them into the woods near a prison in North Alabama, and the other one to this cabin. That's how."

Lucy narrowed her eyes. She knew about the phone. She found it next to Banks's unconscious form and left it in the car. As far as she knew, it was still there. How stupid of her not to turn it off or destroy it.

"I'm telling the truth." Wolfgang relaxed in the chair, but his stare remained intense, switching from Lucy to Banks, then back. "I need to speak to Reed. Where is he?"

Banks looked down, sniffling through her mutilated nose.

Lucy bit her lip, then turned back to Wolfgang.

"We don't know."

8

"I need a gun."

Gambit smirked. "You don't need a gun to break a neck."

The van rolled to a stop next to the curb, and the driver shoved it into park. He was one of the big guys Reed had seen accompanying Gambit—tall, broad, silent—the usual semi-gangster, bodyguard type.

Reed was neither impressed nor intimidated. Everybody dies when their hearts stop or their brains explode, no matter how big or silent they are. He redirected his attention to Gambit sitting in the back of the panel van across from him and raised his hands, rattling the handcuffs.

Gambit twitched the tip of the Glock .45 pointed at Reed's chest, and the driver climbed out of his door and circled the van, opening the rolling side door while Gambit kept the pistol trained on Reed.

"The federal courthouse is four blocks away, near the river," Gambit said. "Perry's office is on the third floor, facing downtown. Sunrise is in about twenty-five minutes. You have twenty to breach the courthouse, complete the kill, and return to the van."

The driver leaned in next to Reed and dug through a toolbox, coming up a moment later with a black ankle monitor on a thick strap. Without a word, he strapped the monitor just above Reed's shoe. It was tight and bit into Reed's skin, but he didn't so much as flinch. He kept his eyes fixed on Gambit, refusing to lose the impromptu staring contest that was triggered the moment they sat across from each other.

"Your new jewelry is there to keep you honest," Gambit said. "If you go anywhere except the courthouse, or if you take too long, or if you decide to get cute and smash it against a brick . . . well, I really don't need to tell you what happens to David."

In Reed's mind, he'd already left the van. He was planning his every step once his feet hit the ground, envisioning an invisible clock in his head that counted steadily down to zero as he dashed for the courthouse. The average block was five or six hundred feet, so it was less than a mile to the courthouse and back. He could easily traverse that distance in seven or eight minutes, which left him twelve to breach the courthouse, reach the third floor . . .

His mind trailed off as the next step in the puzzle confronted him. He didn't want to think about that part yet. He wasn't ready.

"Any questions?"

"Aren't you worried about being caught?" Reed said. "After all, you're my getaway driver."

Gambit smirked. "Why don't you let me worry about that, tough guy?"

Reed shrugged and held up his hands again, shaking the cuffs once more. Gambit held his eye for a moment, then gave the driver a brief nod. A moment later, the cuffs fell away, and Reed resisted the urge to rub his wrists. Ever since prison, he couldn't bear the touch of handcuffs. It was all mental, he knew, but as the steel clicked and closed around his skin, an invisible barrier began to suffocate his mind. It made him want to scream and thrash and do whatever it took to break free.

"All right, Mr. Montgomery." In true villain fashion, Gambit produced a stopwatch and offered a wide grin before smashing the start button. "You're on the clock."

Reed shoved both legs out the door and broke into a run before he was even standing upright. In a moment, he was at full speed, leaping onto the sidewalk and dashing up the hill toward the low skyline that greeted him. He wasn't entirely sure what the courthouse would look like, or if it was even on this street, but he guessed Gambit had no reason to confuse or deceive him. Unless this were some sort of trap designed to place him back in the custody of the FBI—which wouldn't make much sense—Gambit wanted him to proceed to the target as quickly as possible. That would mean no distractions and no time spent searching for the building.

The cold air of an impending Arkansas winter stung his lungs as his legs stretched and he bounded up a gentle hill. Little Rock was only a fraction of the size of Atlanta, but there were still some pretty tall buildings scattered around downtown, mixed with a smattering of politicians and businesspeople starting their day before the sun. All of them could be witnesses or even assailants, should they determine him to be a threat. This was the South, after all. These people carried guns and prided themselves on being sheepdogs of the people. The vast majority of them possessed the tactical ability of a turtle, but a loaded gun is a loaded gun. He would have to move quickly and avoid direct contact.

Another crosswalk flashed beneath his feet, then he saw a tall grey building rising out of the cityscape directly ahead. It had an imperial look to it—narrow windows and thick columns built of solid granite. It was definitely a government building and probably the courthouse. He didn't have time for it to be anything else, so he steered directly for it and lengthened his stride.

Two men in coats coming down the sidewalk stepped aside when they saw Reed, momentary confusion crossing their faces. He burst past them and turned for the main entrance of the building, which he could tell was unlocked as another man in a suit pressed in just ahead of him. Above the door, engraved into the rock in bold letters were the words:

RICHARD   SHEPPARD   ARNOLD   UNITED   STATES COURTHOUSE.

Bingo.

Reed cut his stride short and slipped inside, just behind the man in the suit. A sheriff's deputy stood at a metal detector, his eyes half-open as he nursed a cup of coffee. He took the man in the suit's ID, glanced over it, then waved him through the metal detector. Reed stopped and knelt, making a show of tying his shoe, and allowed the suited man to disappear down the hallway. Then he stood up and rushed forward.

"Slow it down, sir. Court isn't going anywhere. Got your ID?"

Reed felt around his pockets, but he already knew they were empty. The panic he projected onto his face was only half-faked as the clock continued to count down in his head.

"Shit. It's not here. Oh shit, man. I can't find it!"

"Calm down, sir. What's your purpose here?"

"I've got a hearing. That was my lawyer who just passed through. Can you call him back?"

The deputy glanced down the hallway, then sighed and rubbed his eyes.

"All right, buddy. Let me sweep you down, then you go get him."

He ushered Reed through the U-shaped metal detector, then patted him down for a double-check.

"Go get him and come back, okay? Make it quick."

Reed thanked him, then dashed down the hallway. Gambit had said the judge's office faced downtown, which was to his back. That meant he had to find his way three floors up, probably through more security, and then turn around. Maybe there would be directories or something on the wall. He wasn't quite sure where he was on the clock, but he had to be closing in on eight minutes.

His heart pounded, and something in the back of his mouth tasted like blood. Had he bitten his tongue? Around the corner was a bank of elevators with a small crowd of sleepy-eyed people in suits waiting for them. Reed broke through the doorway to the stairs and took them two and three at a time, up two levels, before breaking through a doorway labeled with a bold number three.

This hallway was carpeted, with a lobby on his left and more doorways on his right. He slowed to a jog and caught his breath, moving to his right and checking the directories on each door. None were for Judge Perry.

At the end of the hallway, a window faced westward, with the bulk of downtown to the south. That meant he needed to turn left, but as he passed the window, he caught the glint of impending sunlight reflecting in a nearby tower's windows.

Move it, Reed. Move it.

The next hallway was wide with floral-print carpet and a simple chair rail running down both walls. At the end was a metal door with a rein-forced glass window and a keypad lock. Beside it, a simple wooden sign with brass letters was mounted to the wall:

THE HONORABLE S. J. PERRY

Reed slid to a stop, wiping sweat from his lip as his heart continued to thump.

What now?

He couldn't break the glass or defeat the lock. This was a well-built door. He'd need some C4 or a truck winch to take it down. He didn't have either. He didn't have time. He didn't—

The door handle twisted, and a young man in a black suit and small, round glasses appeared with his arms full of document boxes. With a clean face and bright eyes, he couldn't have been more than twenty-five.

Some kind of aide, Reed thought. Maybe the judge's personal clerk or a law student desperate to make a name for himself.

Reed didn't have time to think or second-guess himself. He dashed forward and pinned the man against the wall with one forearm while he caught the door with his foot. The boxes spilled to the floor and the aide opened his mouth to scream, but Reed clamped his left hand over it, then pinched his right hand over either side of the aide's throat, cutting off his air supply.

The seconds ticked by as the aide struggled against the wall, helpless to break free as his body consumed precious oxygen. It wasn't long before his cheeks flushed and his eyes rolled back. Reed released him and watched as he slumped against the floor, as limp as a wet dishrag.

Reed knelt and checked his pulse. It was still strong, and with a fresh supply of oxygen, it probably wouldn't be long before he was conscious again.

"I'm so sorry," Reed whispered, and then kicked the door open and charged in.

9

The office that greeted him was wide and deep with more narrow windows and a beautiful mahogany desk sitting center stage. The windows faced downtown, just as Gambit had said, and the room was clearly the home office of a legal mastermind. Shelves of thick manuals, boxes of paperwork, and piles of court documents were packed in on every side. Even so, it wasn't a messy room. There was a certain order to it. A pride, even.

Reed took a cautious step forward, then scanned the room a second time. The American flag stood proudly behind the desk, and along the wall were framed diplomas and pictures of people in crisp business attire standing next to each other or shaking hands. It didn't take Reed long to find the judge among the pictures. She was tall, with a wide smile, brown hair, and piercing grey eyes. Not a model's face, but certainly not unpleasant to look at, either. In one photo, she shook hands with what was likely a Supreme Court justice. In another, she stood next to the president. But in the middle of the wall, one photograph stood out, larger than the rest, with a plusher, more expensive frame. It depicted the judge and her family. A tall, thin man with similar brown hair, two adult women and their husbands, and four grandchildren of varying ages. The women were twins, not identical, but definitely favored their mother.

Reed realized he'd stopped cold as he stared at the photograph. He glanced around the room again. A narrow hallway led to what he assumed was the bathroom because he could hear a sink running and somebody speaking in a quiet but animated voice. A moment later, the door swung open, and Reed instinctively drew back into the shadows as Judge Perry appeared from the bathroom, a phone clamped to one ear. She was dressed in a ladies' pantsuit and an unbuttoned jacket, and she smiled with the same intensity he saw in the family portrait.

"Oh, sweetheart, that's so exciting. Did the tooth fairy leave you something under the pillow? He did? Oh . . . oh, no, honey. Twenty is better than twenty-five. It's dollars, not cents."

She laughed, her cheeks flushing a rosy red. And then she saw Reed.

As their gazes met, Reed stood frozen, backed into the corner next to the door. He saw momentary confusion cross her eyes, then panic. She didn't move, just stared, and then slowly lowered the phone and hit the end call button.

Reed felt his heart skip. He hadn't expected that. As soon as she saw him, he expected her to scream and call for help or to tell the child on the phone to get her mother. Something.

But Perry ended the call, almost as if she were protecting the child.

"You're the one the FBI is hunting," she said, her voice strong but not overbearing.

Reed didn't say anything. His heart continued to pound, but his body wouldn't move.

What the hell are you doing? Get it over with. You should've never let her see you. Move! Now!

Something glinted across Perry's stare—recognition, maybe, or perhaps resignation. He wasn't sure.

"You're here to kill me, aren't you?" she asked.

Reed couldn't speak or move, and his throat began to swell, cutting off his air supply.

Do it, dammit. Your father is going to die if you don't. Kill this woman!

With a clenched fist, he took a halting step forward, but Perry didn't retreat or move to shield herself.

Grab her by the neck, pin her against the wall, and deliver one blow to the base of her skull. A quick move. A merciful death.

Reed took another two steps and reached out towards Perry with one hand. He could already envision himself grabbing her by the collar and propelling her against the wall. She was much too weak to resist him. It would be so easy.

But his knees locked, and he stopped. He couldn't move.

What am I doing? This woman has a family. She's done nothing wrong.

In a flash, the faces of each of his victims passed through his mind, beginning with the five dead civilian contractors in Iraq, then moving quickly to the man he killed in prison, followed by all twenty-nine of Oliver's contracts. He could see their faces as clear and crisp as if they were bleeding out on the carpet right in front of him. Their faces faded, and he saw each of the thugs he had gunned down since this war with Aiden had begun.

Those people deserved to die, didn't they? They were men of violence, greed, and destruction. He could think of a reason why killing each of them had been *the right thing to do*. Wasn't that his reason for gunning down those contractors in the first place, all those years ago in Baghdad? It was *the right thing to do*. The thing that nobody else was willing to do.

That was his justification. Or his excuse. He wouldn't allow himself to debate the difference. Either way, regardless of right and wrong, those steps had led him here, to the doorstep of somebody who absolutely didn't deserve to die. Somebody who did nothing wrong.

She wasn't just an innocent woman; she was a good woman and a civil servant.

Reed met her gaze and lowered his hand. He bowed his head a little, just once, and then broke for the door. The aide still lay on the floor, groaning and twisting as Reed leapt over him. A moment later, he crashed into the stairwell, following the signs to the fire escape. Sirens screamed through the courthouse, and he could hear the boots of deputies and security in the hallways, all hurrying to protect the judge.

A wide metal door with a red handle blocked his way on the first floor. Reed shoved through it and crashed onto the sidewalk, then turned north toward the van and stretched into a powerful stride, eating up the yards by the dozens. In only moments, the van pivoted around on the road and was ready to drive. Another two dozen strides and Reed jumped inside, then threw the door shut behind him.

Gambit was in his face before the door even closed, pressing the Glock into Reed's cheek and shouting at him to get on the floor. With a quick twist of his hand, Reed yanked the Glock out of Gambit's hand and dropped the mag. The weapon clattered to the floor in multiple pieces as Reed grabbed Gambit by the shoulders and propelled him into his seat.

The driver slammed on the brakes and swung backward, producing a gun from his jacket. Gambit held up his hand and shook his head, panic flooding his eyes as he faced Reed.

"Listen to me, you little shit." Reed growled the words, spraying Gambit's cheeks with spit. "I don't work for free. If you want the job done, you're going to *pay for it*. Do you understand? I make the kill, and you give me my father. No more games. Are you ready to deal, or not?"

Gambit leaned against the wall, the panic fading as his practiced calm took over. He waved his driver away and sat up, dusting off his shirt.

"All right, then, Montgomery. Let's deal."

10

Banks watched as Lucy continued to interrogate Wolfgang. Half an hour passed, and the sun broke through the trees, but they were no closer to the truth about Wolfgang and Reed.

"He has something I want. That's all I've got to say."

Wolfgang repeated the line like a guilty CEO pleading the Fifth Amendment.

Banks retreated onto the back porch, drawing a deep breath of fresh forest air through dry lips. Her nose throbbed with every beat of her heart, but thanks to Lucy's meds, it didn't hurt as much. She could see clearly and process somewhat-coherent thoughts. That was a huge improvement.

The sliding glass door ground open, then closed behind her, and she heard the soft steps of Lucy approaching.

"How are you feeling?"

Lucy's voice was almost maternal, though she wasn't much older than Banks. Some girls were like that, though. Banks felt pretty maternal about animals, if not about her friends. Did Lucy see her as some kind of pet? Maybe not, but she had definitely assumed a protective attitude toward her.

"I'm okay," Banks said. "My nose hurts."

Lucy leaned against the rail and wiped a wisp of red hair out of her eyes. Banks wondered if the hair was dyed. She thought Lucy looked a bit mousy, with her small stature and narrow features, but graceful, with a wonderful smile.

Banks gazed into the forest again and tried to sniff. A flash of pain rang through her head, and she scowled at herself.

"I never thanked you for . . . saving me, I guess."

Lucy smiled. "You don't have to thank me, honey. To be honest, I was a little late to the show. You were already knocked out when I found you."

"You got the guy who did it?"

Lucy hesitated, then nodded once. "I confronted the perpetrator."

"I had a gun," Banks said. "I should've been able to defend myself."

"Don't feel that way. It takes years of training to adequately defend yourself. And besides, the attacker slipped up on you."

Banks wondered how Lucy knew that. Maybe she was giving her the benefit of the doubt.

"Who are you?" Banks asked. It was the obvious question, but it hadn't seemed overly important until now.

"Well . . ." Lucy brushed hair from her face again.

"My name is Lucy Byrne. I'm an . . . um . . ."

"Assassin for hire."

"Yes."

"You work with Reed."

"Not directly. We shared an employer."

"The bald guy with the bad English accent."

Lucy laughed. "Yes . . . Oliver. Although, he actually *was* British, believe it or not."

"Had me fooled."

"Oliver wasn't a pleasant individual. I doubt anybody is mourning his death."

"I'm not. I killed him."

Lucy looked up. "Really? I thought—"

"That Reed did it? Yeah, maybe he finished him off, I'm not sure, but I shot him in the back. And then . . . I left. It's all kind of a blur."

Lucy nodded but didn't comment. For a moment, everything was almost still, accentuated only by the gentle waft of a breeze through the pines.

Banks fingered her sleeve, then tilted her head to one side. "At the prison . . . in the woods."

"Yes?"

Banks looked at Lucy. "You were there to kill Reed?"

Lucy smiled and brushed her hair back again. "No, I wasn't there to kill anybody. I was there to protect Reed, actually. Years ago, he saved my life. When I found out that Oliver's killers were after him, I decided to step in and do what I could."

Banks grunted and rolled her eyes.

"What?"

"I'll bet there's a whole host of women who have decided to '*do what they can.*' He has that way about him. You get a feeling that maybe he's more than what he looks like and that it would be worth it to find out."

Banks sniffed and looked away. The twist in her stomach tightened, and she remembered what it felt like when he held her. In spite of the grenades, the snowstorm, and almost dying in the woods, when he held her, she felt safe, as though there was an impenetrable wall around her that would deflect anything until the end of time.

That son of a bitch. She believed in him. She *wanted* to believe in him, but in the end, he was so much worse than the average jerk leaning up against the bar, gawking at her while she sang. He was actually, truly, a terrible person.

"About that . . ." Lucy's voice was tentative, almost reluctant.

"About what?"

"About the, um . . . women in Reed's life."

Banks whirled on her, eyes blazing before she could stop herself.

Lucy recoiled a little and held up a hand.

"No, no, not me. I barely knew Reed. I only met him a couple times. What I mean is, he had one known associate—a car thief he met in Europe. There were rumors about it. You have to understand, in Oliver's company, Reed was something of a legend. Everybody respected him. So, his personal life was a topic of interest, especially since so little was known of it."

Banks snapped, "What are you saying?"

"Well, I need you to promise to stay calm and not do anything . . . rash. I feel like you deserve to know this, but I really can't deal with you if you flip out."

"Do I *look* like the kind of woman who would flip out?"

Lucy raised an eyebrow and mimicked Banks's gentle Southern twang. "And I quote, '*I'm a Mississippi redneck, bitch!*'"

Banks made a show of leaning back against the rail and folding her arms, never breaking eye contact with Lucy. She doubted she looked relaxed. With her eggplant of a nose, she doubted she looked anything less than horrific.

"Point taken. But I'm calm now."

Lucy sighed.

"Your attacker in the woods . . . it wasn't a man. It was a woman. I don't know her, and I don't know why she was there. She wasn't one of Oliver's killers. I think she was somebody special to Reed."

Banks's hands trembled, and she jammed them beneath her armpits.

"Banks, what I'm trying to say is, she won't talk to me, but she's hell-bent on finding him. I was hoping you could talk to her."

"Talk to her? She's *here*?"

Lucy nodded. "In the basement."

Banks turned, immediately starting for the steps leading off the deck.

Lucy caught her hand.

"Banks, look at me."

Banks twisted, meeting her gaze with an icy glare.

"I live by a very strict code," Lucy said. "It's part of who I am. One of the things I believe in is repayment in kind. Reed saved my life, and I owe him as much. I tried to talk to her because I want her to quit. If she doesn't, if she insists on hunting him down, well . . . I'll kill her."

Banks pulled away from Lucy's cold grip on her arm, and Lucy didn't fight her. Four steps off the deck, Banks pivoted and found the entrance to the storm cellar. She flung it open, revealing a yellow light, and took the steps two at a time, her head pounding as hard as her heart as she reached the concrete floor and turned into the basement.

A woman sat on a wooden chair, her arms taped behind her back and her ankles secured to the chair legs. She wore a heavy black Middle East-ern–type robe, but her bowed head was exposed.

Banks stopped, her feet scraping against the concrete, and the woman looked up.

The breath whistled between Banks's teeth as if somebody had kicked her in the stomach. The woman's face was something out of a horror movie —the skin scalded, with her lip twisted into a permanent sneer that exposed two of her teeth. One cheek was swollen like a chipmunk with a nut in its mouth while the other was constricted against her jawline. Her hair was burnt and patchy, exposing a crimson scalp.

But her eyes were alive with fire, as clear and vibrant as a teenager's, blasting menace at Banks. A clear, unfiltered threat.

Banks took a cautious step forward, and her hand trembled as she reached out. The woman recoiled, but she couldn't move far. Banks touched the gag wrapped around the woman's head and gently pulled it out.

The woman swallowed and sat perfectly still, like a dog poised to lunge. Banks retracted her still-shaking hand, and for a full minute, neither one of them spoke. Banks wondered if the prisoner could speak. Had the accident, or whatever terrible thing had befallen her, made her mute?

New tears bubbled up, but Banks couldn't stop them. She couldn't bear to see another human being brutalized this way. Had Reed done this to her? Had Reed hurt her this way?

No. Banks couldn't believe it. She refused to believe it.

She wiped the tears from her face, careful to avoid touching her nose, then sat down on the concrete and crossed her legs.

"Hi," she whispered. "I'm Banks."

11

"The target's name is Margaret Trousdale. She goes by Maggie, or Muddy Maggie. She's the governor of Louisiana."

Gambit waited for Montgomery to blink or show any surprise at all, but he didn't. He again sat at the table in the darkened room, unrestrained this time, with his arms crossed.

"Nothing?" Gambit asked, tilting his head to one side. The churning hurricane in his stomach sent another wave of nausea through his body, but he avoided reacting. Montgomery couldn't know how unsteady he felt.

Montgomery failed the test. He didn't kill the judge or harm a hair on her head. And yet, Gambit had no choice but to proceed with the primary assignment. Montgomery called his bluff, and there wasn't much Gambit could do about it. His back was against a wall now.

He could only pray that Montgomery pulled up short on the judge because he wasn't being paid like he claimed, not because he questioned Gambit's judgment. Because if that were the case . . .

Gambit couldn't worry about possibilities anymore. Shortly after Montgomery fumbled the job in Little Rock, Gambit had finally found a suitable replacement to fill Trousdale's office after her impending death. Somebody who was morally flexible and willing to be a team player. That was a major step forward, and good news for Aiden's operation, but it only mattered if Trousdale were eliminated on schedule. Gambit needed to concentrate on motivating Montgomery.

"Why do you want her dead?" Montgomery's question was flat and toneless. It was the question Gambit hoped he wouldn't ask because it reflected depth of perception on Montgomery's part. Gambit wanted The Prosecutor to view this hit two-dimensionally—the target and the prize: kill Trousdale and get his father back.

A third dimension involving *why* questions dramatically increased the likelihood that Montgomery would go rogue. Should he brush it off and tell Montgomery to mind his own business? Or should he lie, come up with a morally justifiable reason why Trousdale should die, and hope that Montgomery believed him?

What did Oliver do? How did he motivate this mastermind of the kill to do his job and think two-dimensionally?

Gambit had no idea. He clenched his teeth and dug his fingers into the edge of the table. The stress that radiated through his body was reaching a fever pitch, but there wasn't much he could do about it. Could Montgomery see past the charade?

"Governor Trousdale isn't what she seems, Reed. My employer is engaged in some sub-legal business ventures, it's true. Aren't we all?"

Gambit forced a laugh. It sounded insincere, even to him. "But my employer does a lot of good in the world. An entire wing of his company is dedicated to researching and manufacturing life-saving medication, believe it or not. You know how the pharmaceutical world can be, though. So many layers of red tape holding back the progress of drugs that people are desperate to buy. Drugs that people *need*. Governor Trousdale comes from a poor family. She's leveraging the power of her office against my employer, threatening to apply new regulations and restrictions. She's trying to shut down his ability to manufacture the medications our customers need unless we pay her bribe, which we could do, of course. But does a person deserve to be congratulated for threatening the lives of thousands of others? My employer doesn't think so."

Again, Montgomery didn't move. Gambit had no idea if he was buying the story or not, and it was maddening. It made him want to sling the table into The Prosecutor's face, then bludgeon him with a chair.

Gambit sat on the edge of the table and folded his arms. "It's a priority for my employer that Governor Trousdale meet a quick and conspicuous end, and for that, he is willing not only to give you your father but also the multi-million-dollar bribe that Trousdale demanded. He's a generous man, Reed. It's not about the money."

Montgomery offered a bone-chilling smirk. "I've worked on the wrong side of the law for a long time, Gambit. It's *always* about the money."

Gambit licked his lips and forced himself not to become defensive. It wouldn't help.

"Reed, I'm not here to compare moral rap sheets with you. It's my understanding that you have quite the checkered past yourself. You're no stranger to taking the shot when the money is right. Well, the money is right. Very right. So, let's stop with the banter and get down to business."

Montgomery grunted. "Where is she?"

"Baton Rouge, usually. About a six-hour drive from here."

"Security?"

"I've outlined everything we know about her schedule, her habits, and her security detail in this brief. It's pretty comprehensive."

Gambit produced a bulging envelope from his coat and laid it on the table. Montgomery picked it up but didn't open it.

"Do we have a deal, Reed?"

Montgomery tapped the envelope against the table.

"I'll need some equipment."

"Of course. Whatever you need."

"You should take notes."

Gambit pursed his lips but produced his phone from his coat and opened the notes app. "Okay, Mr. Montgomery, may I take your order?"

"One SIG Sauer P226 handgun with five magazines loaded with +P hollow points made in America. No Chinese or Russian shit. One Springfield M1A Scout Squad rifle, with five twenty-round magazines filled with ballistic-tip, match-grade ammunition. American made. One Burris 200261 Ballistic Plex optic, brand-new, in the box. I better not find one damn fingerprint on it."

Gambit paused over the phone and cleared his throat. "*Is that all?*"

"I also need five grand in small bills. And I need a car."

Gambit nodded, jotting down the additional note. "Not a problem. I can get you something nondescript. A Ford, or—"

"I want a brand-new BMW M2 Competition Coupe, black-on-black, manual transmission. No sunroof. Louisiana license plates and local registration."

"Not *American made*?"

"I don't know, Gambit. Where do they make BMW?"

Gambit leaned back and folded his arms.

"Look, *buddy*. It must be difficult to talk to me from that high, high horse of yours, but I'm not a vending machine. I'll get you what you need. I'm not buying your dream car."

"You can't afford my dream car. The Beemer will do."

"You seriously think I'm dropping forty grand on a new BMW for you to wrap around a pole?"

"No, I think you're dropping sixty grand on a BMW that I can do literally anything I want with because I'm the man for the job, and like you said, *the money is right*."

Gambit held his glare on Montgomery, testing the waters, waiting to see if Montgomery was jerking his chain and seeing how much he could get away with. He couldn't tell, and that was the most infuriating thing about Montgomery. Unless Gambit could knock The Prosecutor off-kilter—which took *a lot*—he had no way of knowing what this big killer was thinking.

"Fine," Gambit said. "I'll see what I can do."

Montgomery leaned forward and interlaced his fingers. "You'll get me what I asked for, down to the last detail. And then you'll get the hell out of my way."

12

"How long have you known Lieutenant Governor Sharp?"

Maggie cleared her throat and ran a hand across her mouth. It wasn't a complex question, but it was still difficult to process.

"My whole life, I guess. His father owns a Chrysler dealership in my hometown. He was a family friend."

The man sitting across from her had thick black hair and the piercing eyes of a person who was used to having these sorts of conversations. Director Jerod Brewer of the Louisiana Bureau of Investigation was a terrifying man, and that wasn't just because he was sitting in her office, asking probing questions about her recently disgraced LG. Brewer had a commanding severity about him that made you believe he was going to sniff out the truth no matter how deep it was buried.

He was a bloodhound with a giant virtual snout that could smell a lie a mile away.

"How would you describe Sharp's relationship with the late Attorney General Matthews?"

Maggie's stomach conducted a somersault. She glanced across the room to where Coulier sat, his fingers steepled beneath his nose. He gave her a reassuring nod.

Brewer caught the exchange, and his eyes narrowed, sending another wave of nausea ripping through Maggie's body. Did he suspect something? Was he onto them?

It probably wasn't a good idea for Coulier to be here. Maybe it was making Brewer suspicious. But in a strange way, Maggie was reassured by Coulier's presence. He'd disappeared the day before. Nobody was sure where he went. But when Coulier returned, his demeanor had shifted. He was more confident. More reassuring. Enough so that she had agreed to the "formality" of being interviewed by Brewer.

Maybe that was a mistake.

"Madam Governor?"

Maggie realized she hadn't answered Brewer's most recent question. She cleared her throat, stalling for time.

"I'm not sure how well Sharp knew Matthews. I mean, they worked together for only a few months before, well . . ."

"Before AG Matthews passed away."

"Yes."

"Did they collaborate on any projects? Any specific investigations?"

Maggie searched her tired brain, looking for a bone to throw the investigator—something true but innocuous. This interview had been going on for over an hour, and she just wanted him to leave.

"I can't think of anything. I mean, Sharp and I were trying to find our feet back then. There was so much going on. It's difficult to remember."

Brewer nodded but didn't look away. She couldn't tell if he was suspicious or bored.

"In your official statement regarding Lieutenant Governor Sharp, Madam Governor, you wrote, quote: 'Over the past six months, Sharp has demonstrated increasingly hostile behavior toward the administration, has spent prolonged periods of time in insolation, and has been negligent in his duties.' Would you elaborate on that, ma'am?"

Maggie stared at the director and swallowed. The quote was from the statement that Coulier prepared, and once again, she cursed herself for signing it without reading it. There were things like *this* in the document—

accusations and claims that were bold, unqualified, and almost hostile. Accusations that she would now have to back up.

Given the fact that they were all untrue, substantiating them was proving to be a nightmare. She had to think of a way to qualify her claims without stating anything objective enough to be disproven.

"Dan was . . ." She hesitated. "He was distant. Distracted. I felt like there was something on his mind."

Brewer grunted and directed his stare at his notepad.

"Could you describe what you meant by *'negligent in his duties'*? What duties, specifically, was LG Sharp negligent in?"

It was all Maggie could do not to scream. She felt backed into a corner, as though drooling dogs were breathing down her neck and demanding answers.

This was her *friend*. Dan was her closest confidant, and she was lying about him. Destroying him.

Her hand began to shake.

She couldn't do it anymore. She couldn't lie about Dan. What the hell had she become?

Coulier spoke from the corner of the room. "Mr. Director. . . ."

Brewer looked up as Coulier stepped toward them.

"Mr. Attorney General?"

"Governor Trousdale is exhausted, and as I'm sure you can understand, emotionally strained. It's been a tremendously difficult time for us all. Perhaps we can postpone the remainder of this interview for early tomorrow?"

Brewer didn't look at all happy with the arrangement, but in an indirect way, Coulier was Brewer's boss. This wasn't going to be a debate.

Brewer stood and turned back to Maggie.

"Madam Governor, as I'm sure you know, the LBI would typically be happy to keep your office apprised of our investigations. However, since this investigation involves the executive office itself, I'm afraid that is not practicable. I will be reporting directly to the attorney general on this matter."

Maggie nodded, barely hearing the words. She didn't care who Brewer reported to. She didn't care what happened next. Why did it matter? She'd betrayed her friend and stabbed him right in the back without a second thought. Nothing else mattered.

Coulier escorted Brewer out of the room, then shut the doors. He stood with his back to Maggie for a moment, then let out a sigh and took off his glasses. As he walked back to her desk, he pinched the bridge of his nose and crashed into the chair Brewer had occupied only moments before.

"I thought he'd never shut up," Coulier muttered. "The man in insatiable."

Maggie sniffed, then rubbed the back of her hand across each cheek. "He's going to find out, Coulier. He's going to know what we did."

"And what did we do, Madam Governor?"

"You know what we did. We lied about Dan. We poisoned the—"

"Maggie." Coulier leaned forward, folding his hands. "You must be so exhausted. You're confusing facts. Dan poisoned the harbor. Dan set you up. And I'm not certain"—Coulier sighed—"that he didn't actually kill AG Matthews."

"What the hell are you talking about? Gambit's people did that!"

"Gambit . . ." Coulier offered a tired smile, tapping his glasses against the arm of his chair. "You mean the man you say you met. The man nobody can find."

Maggie sat forward. "What are you saying, Coulier? Are you calling me crazy?"

"Of course not, Maggie. You're a strong woman, dedicated and relentless. Exactly the kind of woman I'm honored to work for. The kind of woman I'd like to report to as lieutenant governor."

The room fell deathly silent, and Maggie's back stiffened. "What?"

Coulier spread his hands. "Think about it. You need me by your side, now more than ever. The Louisiana State Constitution stipulates that in the event of a vacancy in the office of lieutenant governor, the governor should nominate a candidate for the legislature to confirm. This is an unprecedented opportunity to consolidate your power."

"My power? Is that what you're concerned about? Consolidating power?"

"Maggie, I know this is difficult to face right now, but the reality remains. You are the chief executive of the state, and the state needs you. It may be that our enemies were not who we thought they were. It may be that they were much closer to us than we imagined. That makes your mission to lead this state out of the shadow of corruption more important than ever. The people *need you*. Let me stand by your side. I have never failed you, and I won't fail you now."

Maggie slumped in her chair, her head spinning like it was suspended on a demented carnival ride. What was happening? Was Coulier really bidding to be her LG? It made no sense. He was a lawyer. A shrewd, ruthless lawyer with a personal vendetta against some businesses operating in Louisiana. That was the only reason he took the job as her attorney general in the first place: he craved power to avenge himself. Sure, that set off some red flags for Maggie, but she, too, was at war with an invisible force of corruption, and Coulier's vicious approach to prosecution appealed to her.

Why would he want to be LG? It took him away from the legal branch and away from the most direct path to vengeance. Less power, less control. Was this man insane?

Maggie rubbed the heel of her hand against her forehead. A muck of memories swarmed her. It was Coulier, not Sharp, who suggested closing the port. Sharp had objected, adamantly, and wanted nothing to do with the scheme. Hadn't he fought Coulier every step of the way?

She sat up. "Listen to me very carefully, Coulier. You are, at best, an incompetent attorney general. At worst, you're actually corrupt."

"Maggie . . ."

"*Madam Governor!*" She smacked the desk with her open palm. "Don't play me for a fool, Coulier. It was you who suggested I close the port. You who isolated me from Dan. I don't know what kind of game you're playing, but if you think I'm about to nominate you as my new LG in the midst of this shit show, you've got another think coming."

Coulier pushed his glasses up. "Madam Governor, I'm truly grieved to hear you say that. I've worked tirelessly to prosecute your anti-corruption agenda, and I stand by my work. My suggestion that I be nominated was merely a thought. You're right, though. It wouldn't serve you best. I apologize for being so bold, and I apologize for being so familiar. I only meant to comfort you."

Maggie felt suddenly unsure of herself. She didn't expect Coulier to back down, let alone apologize. Had she come on too strong?

"Coulier, I'm sorry. I didn't mean that so harshly. It's just—"

"Just a lot going on, Madam Governor. I understand completely."

Coulier stood and offered her a reassuring smile. "I'm here when you need me, ma'am. For as long as you need me."

He started toward the door, then paused and glanced back. "If I may . . . I do have one small suggestion, something that I think would soothe the tension around here."

Maggie looked up. "Yes?"

"Take a trip down to New Orleans this week. Go to the harbor and conduct a press conference. You can reopen the port and give a speech. Remind the people why they elected you. I think it could be good . . . for everyone. Just a thought."

"That's an excellent idea. Thank you."

Coulier bowed slightly, then disappeared through the doors. As they clapped shut behind him, an icy draft washed across her skin, and Maggie shivered.

For the first time in her life, she was truly, absolutely alone.

13

The sun rose well over the trees before Banks emerged from the basement. Her body ached with exhaustion, and her face was streaked with tears, but the sunlight felt good on her skin, like the kiss of heaven.

She turned back and opened the second door, then held out her hand. Kelly took it and followed her up the steps and onto the porch. The shorter woman cast a wary glance around the property, no doubt looking for Lucy, but Banks gave her hand a soft squeeze.

"Don't worry. Nobody's going to hurt you."

The ice in Kelly's glare melted for a moment as she faced Banks, and she nodded. Banks pulled the sliding glass door open and stepped inside the living room.

Wolfgang was still tied to the chair, his face a cross between disgust and simple boredom. He looked up when they entered and grimaced when he saw Kelly. Banks shin-kicked him.

"Ouch! I'm sorry! I didn't expect . . . to see that."

Banks led Kelly to the couch and motioned for her to sit down.

"Are you hungry?"

Kelly nodded again, and Banks walked into the kitchen. She could hear the shower running in the background, mixed with the gentle soprano of a woman singing Bob Hope. Lucy had a great voice—unassuming but confident. Banks glanced back into the living room to see that Wolfgang was nodding his head to the song, a gentle smile framing his face.

Outstanding. Everybody here is a lunatic.

She found bread and peanut butter in the pantry and made two sandwiches, then poured milk from the fridge into a plastic cup and walked back into the living room.

Kelly stared hungrily at the plate but waited until Banks sat down before accepting it. Banks sat and smiled, watching her gulp down the food. The first sandwich was gone in seconds, and Kelly wiped her mouth with the back of her hand before giving the second sandwich a greedy glance.

Banks pushed the plate her way. "Go ahead. I made it for you."

Wolfgang grunted from the chair a couple feet away. "Don't worry about me. I'm full, actually. Just ate a steak dinner. Ribeye, eight ounce. I'm not a pig."

Kelly sneered at him and picked up the sandwich, taking a slow and dramatic bite.

"Everything about you is cruel and unusual punishment," Wolfgang muttered.

The shower cut off, but the song continued. Lucy was moving through Hope's biggest hits, selecting some of Banks's favorites. She remembered what it felt like to sing—what it felt like to enjoy a song and get lost in the music and not be burdened by the weight of the world crushing down on her soul. It had only been a few weeks since she sat on that stool at the club in Atlanta. It felt like years.

Sirena Wilder was her stage name. She remembered what it felt like to be Sirena—always broke, usually lonely, and exclusively semi-depressed. But Sirena was never on the run for her life. Never at a loss for anything except the next meal.

Banks looked down at her bruised hands and sighed. She didn't feel like singing now and wasn't sure if she would ever feel like singing again.

Maybe Sirena was dead, a casualty of this strange, brutal world she found herself lost in.

Footsteps tapped in the hallway, mixed with a gentle whistle. The whistle stopped abruptly, and Banks heard the metallic shriek of Lucy's sword clearing its scabbard.

"What the hell?"

Banks spoke without looking up. "Put it away, Lucy. She was hungry."

Lucy took a cautious step into the living room. She wore a towel wrapped around her torso, which would've been too short on both ends for Banks, but encapsulated Lucy like a burrito. Her red hair dripped from between her shoulder blades, and she held out the blade toward Kelly.

"She's dangerous, Banks," Lucy said. "I shouldn't have to tell you that."

"*Put it away*, now!" Banks snapped. "Kelly isn't going to hurt anyone."

"I concur," Wolfgang said. "Honestly, tying people up in general is barbaric—"

Lucy backhanded him across the face, and Wolfgang blinked as though he'd just been hit by a fly swatter.

"Relax, Spider-Chick," Kelly muttered, her voice hoarse but clear. "I learned my lesson about fighting you. You can put the cheese knife away."

Lucy lowered the blade and backed across the room, settling into a chair across from the couch. She crossed her ankles, her attention fixated on Kelly until she caught sight of Wolfgang staring at her exposed knees. She flicked the blade toward him, and Wolfgang winced.

"Please don't!" he said.

Kelly snorted a short laugh. "Who the hell is this dweeb?"

Banks walked into the kitchen and found bread to make more sandwiches.

"He calls himself Wolfgang Pierce."

"Wolfgang Pierce. Sounds made up as hell," Kelly said. "What are you in for, Mr. Pierce? Cross up with Spider-Chick, did you?"

"Stop calling me that," Lucy snapped. "It's belittling."

"Well, you kinda look like a Spider-Chick. Skintight leather, moves like a cat, and the sword."

"More like a samurai," Wolfgang muttered.

Lucy rolled her eyes. "Samurai were men, you moron. I'm just a sassy redhead with a blade."

Kelly grunted. "Spider-Chick, like I said."

Lucy raised the sword, but Banks reappeared into the room with a plateful of sandwiches. She set them on the coffee table, then selected one and plopped down on the couch. "Will all of you shut the hell up, please? God, you're like a bunch of old people at an ice cream social."

Lucy and Kelly exchanged wary glances, then they leaned forward and lifted sandwiches off the plate, retreating immediately back to their seats and still glaring at each other.

"So, about that steak . . ." Wolfgang said, licking his lips. "There weren't any sides."

Lucy sighed and flicked her sword. The tip sliced through the tape that restrained Wolfgang's right hand, passing only a millimeter from his skin but leaving him without a scratch.

"If you so much as twitch the wrong way, you'll lose your head."

Wolfgang tore his arm free and stretched for a sandwich. "You know, you're kinda sexy with that blade."

Lucy ignored him, and for a moment, all four of them were silent as the sandwiches faded from the plate. Kelly leaned back and belched so loud Banks thought she heard the windowpanes rattle. Banks shot her a surprised glance.

Kelly shrugged. "What? It's not like I've got a dainty image to protect."

Red tinged the edges of Kelly's dark eyes, and she looked down at her hands.

Banks decided not to say anything, and instead, finished her sandwich. The room was silent again, but this time there was the definite air of uncertainty in it, as though everyone was waiting for somebody else to make the first move.

Banks decided to take control before Lucy did something provocative with the sword.

"Now that everybody has met, I think we can agree that we're all here because of Reed."

The tension in the room skyrocketed, and Banks shifted on the couch and wiped her mouth with the back of her hand.

"Lucy, you were trying to protect him. Wolfgang, you say he has something you need. And Kelly, well . . ."

"I want to carve his heart out," Kelly finished, her tone deathly cold.

Lucy sat up, and the sword clicked against her armrest.

"That's not gonna happen, honey."

Kelly sneered. "What's your angle, Spider-Chick? Another girlfriend?"

Lucy bristled. "Reed is an associate of mine. He saved my life, so I'm returning the favor. Clear enough for you, pumpkin?"

"Honey, pumpkin . . . what are you, Aunt Bee?"

"You really like to call people names, don't you?" Lucy's voice was layered with ice.

"Not always, but when I do, I don't sound like a backwoods redneck with three teeth in her head."

Lucy sat up, the sword already rising. Banks leapt to her feet and held out both hands. "Stop it, both of you! I don't care what your angles are, you're only hurting people!"

"Easy for you to say," Kelly snapped, her voice trembling with emotion. "Your house didn't burn down around your ears. You didn't watch your fiancé roast to death right next to you. You didn't . . ."

Kelly broke off, her voice sounding thick and weak. Her hands broke out into a series of tremors, and she settled back into the chair, tears spilling down her cheeks.

Banks glowered at Lucy until the redhead settled back into her chair.

"Give me the sword," she said, holding out her hand. Lucy shook her head, and Banks stamped her foot against the floor. "*Give me the sword!*"

Lucy flinched, then reluctantly held out the weapon, handle first. Banks took it and placed it in the kitchen, then returned to the living room.

"Look, I hate Reed, too. He hurt me . . . deeply. He's destroyed my whole life. But there's a bigger picture here."

Banks spent the next few minutes walking the three of them through everything that had happened since she met Reed: the kidnapping in Atlanta, the train, the events in the mountains, the gunfight with Oliver Enfield, and then Nashville—the hidden fraternity, their dark secrets, and their lost members.

She concluded with confronting Dick Carter in Wyoming before jour-
neying back to Alabama to find David Montgomery.

"I was working with Reed because I need to know what happened to my
daddy." Her voice trembled, but she kept going. "He was everything to me,
and he was stolen. I don't believe he was killed by a drunk driver. I have to
know the truth, and then I have to crush the man responsible. Reed was
helping me get there."

Silence filled the room. Lucy stared at Banks with a sympathetic pucker
of her lips, and Kelly just glared at the wall. Her hands continued to tremble, the endless nuisance of her damaged nerves. But there was more to it,
also.

Kelly bolted to her feet and snapped. "So you lost your *daddy*? I lost
everything! Sing your sad song someplace else, *bitch*!"

Lucy jumped up, already moving to intercept Kelly as the deranged
woman flung herself at Banks. The room filled with all three of their
screams as Wolfgang slung himself sideways, crashing to the floor out of
their way. Kelly's first blow rocketed toward Banks's nose but was deflected
at the last moment as Lucy head-butted her in the ribs. The three women
clattered to the floor, sending the plate spinning across the room. Fists, legs,
and three colors of hair mixed in a swirl as punches were slung and teeth
were bared. Banks felt a knee slam into her stomach, knocking the air out
of her. She rolled free as the ceiling spun overhead, then she landed on her
side and saw Kelly hit the floor on top of Lucy, her right fist drawn back,
ready for a punch.

"Don't!" Banks shouted.

The punch started to fall. Kelly leaned forward, gritting her teeth,
aiming straight for Lucy's china-doll face.

Then, a low whimper rang out from down the hallway, and toenails
clicked on the hardwood. Kelly stopped cold, mid-blow, and looked up.
Feet pattered across the hardwood, followed by another whimper.

Kelly's hand fell to her side, and she whispered, "Baxter?"

Reed's old bulldog erupted into a gallop, busting out of the hallway
with a happy yelp. He jumped over Lucy's head and fell into Kelly's lap. The
two tumbled to the floor as the dog continued to bark and lick Kelly's disfigured face.

Banks hauled herself to her feet, then helped Lucy up. The redhead started toward Kelly, but Banks held her back.

"Wait," she whispered. "Look . . ."

Kelly sat on the floor, her arms wrapped around the dog in a bear hug as she leaned into his shoulder and sobbed like a child.

14

It took Gambit most of the day to secure the items on Reed's wish list. The pistol, rifle, ammunition, and cash were the easiest. The car took longer. Reed expected that and was even surprised when Gambit hauled him out of the underground bunker and into the fading light of a setting sun to a brand-new BMW M2 parked under the shade of Arkansas trees.

It was the exact model Reed had specified—a Competition Coupe with a twin-turbo six-cylinder engine producing 405 horsepower. Not so raw or loud as his Camaro, but plenty quick. The car was equipped with a six-speed manual transmission, black interior matched to the exterior, and Louisiana license plates. No sunroof.

Gambit tossed him the keys and offered a dry smirk. "Don't wreck it, Reed."

"I'll do whatever I want, Gambit. It's my car."

Inside the trunk, Reed found the rifle waiting in a foam case. It was new, but somebody had already disassembled it and cleaned away all the factory grease. Shorter than a regular M1A, the Scout Squad was a semi-automatic battle rifle chambered in the heavy-hitting .308 Winchester. Normally, Reed would've preferred a custom-built AR-10–style modular rifle for any precision shooting needs, but he neither trusted Gambit to competently construct one, nor did he have the time to wait. Out of the box, the M1A Scout Squad was accurate out to three hundred yards or so, equipped with the Burris long-eye relief scope that was carefully packaged in another box, as instructed. Three hundred yards would be plenty for what Reed needed to do.

He checked the canvas bag next to the rifle case and found the SIG handgun, along with magazines for both weapons, loaded with the ammunition he requested.

"Are you satisfied?" Gambit asked.

Reed shut the trunk and motioned to his leg. "The monitor. Take it off."

Gambit laughed. "I don't think so. We still need to keep an eye on you, after all. And if the monitor goes off course or offline, well, you know what happens."

Reed glared him down, then climbed into the car.

"You have three days, Reed. Don't disappoint me."

Gambit shut the door, and Reed gunned the motor, turning south.

Two hours later, a blue road sign welcomed him to the Pelican State. Reed swerved around a semitruck and took the next exit, steering toward a truck stop. There was plenty of gas in the Beemer's tank, but there was something else he needed.

The little car bounced between trucks on its way to the pump, where Reed topped it off with premium gas before walking inside. Peeling out a hundred-dollar bill from Gambit's supply of running money, Reed purchased a sandwich, a bottle of water, and a prepaid burner phone— something he could communicate with outside the scope of Gambit's knowledge. Then he piloted back onto the highway and turned south.

He would start in Baton Rouge, find the governor, and get a bearing on her activities. Gambit would be watching carefully, and he might even have people on the ground. That would be annoying but not detrimental. If all of Gambit's men were tall, broad, and as dumb as rocks like the ones in Arkansas, Reed would see them coming a mile away.

He powered on the phone, allowed it to cycle through its setup process, then punched in a number from memory.

"Jose's Greek Gods for hire. This is Jose."

"T-Rex, it's Reed."

"Prosecutor, baby! How the hell are you? Still keeping up with that sexy mama?"

Reed sighed. T-Rex was his go-to arms dealer—a loud, obnoxious, and altogether annoying individual who drew enough attention to invite a federal invasion. Yet he slipped enough hardware in and out of Mexico to lay down a National Guard installation.

T-Rex was a study in the oxymoron and the poster boy for any politician who wanted to impose stricter border regulations. Reed wasn't sure he trusted him, but he could certainly rely on him to deliver. To that end, T-Rex had never failed.

"I'm getting along, T-Rex." Reed dodged the loaded question about Banks. T-Rex met her at their last encounter, and it was no secret that he harbored a powerful, if strictly physical, crush. Not that Reed could fault him for his good taste. "I'm calling because—"

"You need something. Of course. You know I got you, baby. What can T-Rex get you today? I picked up some nice automatics last night. Israeli stuff, no numbers."

"Actually, I was looking for something a little more explosive."

T-Rex chuckled. "Oh, you need the *boom-boom*, eh? You know I got you. What kind, and how much?"

"C4. And . . . a lot."

"C4, eh? Hmm. I got some in stock, I think. Medium-grade from Mexico. A bit dirty. Smokes a lot."

"That's perfect. I'll take ten pounds."

T-Rex erupted into a string of Spanish cursing, and the phone hit the floor. A moment later, he retrieved it. "Ten *pounds*? What the hell are you up to, Prosecutor?"

"The usual. Chaos, en masse. Can you hook me up?"

"You know I can, baby. But seriously, that's a lot of juice. Better be careful."

"I know what I'm doing, Rex. I'll take the ten pounds, a remote detonator and, well, this might be a lot to ask, but . . ."

Reed let the comment hang, and he heard T-Rex sniff derisively.

"What, you think I ain't got it? Baby, if it can be *got*, T-Rex can get it. What do you need?"

"It's just, you know, I was hoping you could deliver long distance."

"What, truck it for you across state lines? You're a crazy mother, Reed. No doubt!"

"I'll pay extra. It's not that far. You've moved stuff for me before."

"Sure I have. Guns and ammo, some grenades maybe. But ten pounds of C4?"

"I need it in Baton Rouge. Tomorrow morning, if at all possible. I'll give you three grand."

T-Rex sighed. His ego was taking over, just as Reed hoped.

"You know, if it can be done, T-Rex can do it. But baby, only T-Rex would love you this way . . . you know what I'm saying? Going out on a limb for you, bro."

"You're the best, Rex. Truly. The shit."

"Don't flatter me. I mean, if you wanted to show me some love, you could always hook me up with that sexy señorita you been hanging out with. I mean, baby, she *fine!*"

Reed sighed. "Call me on this number when you're close. We can meet north of the city. Before sunrise would be ideal."

"You got it. I'll catch you soon."

Reed hung up and tossed the phone into the seat. He ran a tired hand across his face and tried not to think about the last few days. He tried not to think about Banks.

He could still see her in the car, in the moments before he left to find David. He never thought that would be the last time they spoke. He couldn't even remember what he said to her. Probably something about being careful and staying safe. Something cautious and distant. None of the things he longed to say to her.

Banks didn't want to hear the things he longed to say. The only thing she wanted was the head of the man who killed her father, and that was what he set out into the woods to find.

And then things changed like they do sometimes. He saw his own father, and for the first time in his life, he realized that he needed that man more than he needed anyone else. There was a chance to break David

Montgomery free. A chance to reunite what was left of Reed's shattered family. He was going to move Heaven and Earth to make that happen.

The BMW's headlights flashed against the oncoming street signs as Reed leaned back in the seat and settled in for the drive. Up ahead, one sign stood out among the rest.

BATON ROUGE. 289 MILES.

15

Kelly spent the next couple hours with Baxter, sitting on the floor and stroking the dog until he fell asleep. A sizable pool of drool formed under his snout as he snored, his wrinkled old body trembling with every breath.

Banks wondered what his story was. Reed had never really said. She thought it odd for a freelance assassin who hid himself from the world and was often away from home—wherever home was—to keep a dog. What was even odder was the breed. Baxter was adorable but useless for any security purpose. He was a pet, nothing more.

What did that say about Reed? The fact that he kept a useless pet around, nurtured it, and was obviously close to it?

What did it say about her that he left Baxter with her?

Banks closed her eyes and once more thought back to the burner phone Lucy had brought in from the car. On it was a single, unread text message. Reed's final words.

I'M GOING. DON'T FOLLOW. TAKE CARE OF BAXTER FOR ME. I KNOW YOU SAID NOT TO SAY IT, BUT I LOVE YOU. GOODBYE.

When Banks opened her eyes, they stung. Lucy sat across from her, staring, and Banks looked away. She wasn't sure what to make of Lucy. Her simple explanation that she turned up out of nowhere to protect Reed made sense, but Banks didn't trust the simple or the obvious anymore. A few weeks before, she would've trusted a panhandler if he said he needed to borrow her debit card only to buy lunch. She was like that. She believed in people. Saw the best in them, even when all available evidence pointed to the opposite.

But now . . .

Kelly got up, sliding the sleeping dog off her lap and onto the floor. He didn't wake up as she walked across the room and settled onto the couch next to Banks. Kelly brushed frazzled strands of hair behind her ear and folded her arms. The ice was still in her eyes, but her body was relaxed, save for the constant tremble in her hands.

"Okay. So what now?"

Banks bit her lip, then turned toward Lucy.

Lucy shrugged, one leg crossed over her knee as she toyed with her shoelace. She wore black high-top converse shoes, and Banks couldn't help but be jealous of them. She had left all her shoes—the only nice things she owned—in Atlanta.

Nobody spoke, and Banks directed her attention to Wolfgang. Lucy had reaffixed his right hand to the chair after he ate the sandwich, and he now sat glaring at the wall as if it were to blame for world hunger.

He must need to pee, Lucy thought. *He's been tied to that chair for a long time.*

"I'm going after Reed," Banks said. "He owes me answers. And, well, I've got nothing else to do. The rest of you can do whatever you want. You don't owe me anything."

Lucy and Kelly were locked in a death stare, both tensed as if they were prepared to leap for each other's throats at any moment.

Kelly spoke first, keeping her eyes on Lucy.

"I'm going with you. I'm not finished with Reed, either."

Lucy shook her head. "Not happening, sister."

"What's your angle?" Kelly snapped. "Why do you care what happens to him?"

Lucy remained unfazed. "He saved my life, so I owe him. It's that simple."

"Ha. Karma, is it? Keeping the universe in balance."

"Yes, actually," Lucy said. "That's it exactly."

Kelly folded her arms. "Well, if karma's your game, I've got some of my own to settle."

Lucy shrugged. "Every girl must try."

"Oh, I'll try. And if you get in my way again, I'll split your pretty little head wide open."

Lucy's back stiffened, but before she could retort, Banks stepped between them and held up both hands. "Stop! Just stop. We're not starting this again. I'm going. If you're coming, fine, but the fighting has to stop. We're not enemies here!"

Both women looked sheepishly at each other, then Kelly nodded, and Lucy's shoulders relaxed.

"Look, I'm inspired by the girl band, really," Wolfgang said, "but all of you are getting in the way of something much more important than *karma*. So, if you'll untie me from this chair, I'll lock your asses in the basement and be on my way."

Banks turned on him, glowering. She leaned down and stuck a stiff finger into his ribcage. Wolfgang grimaced.

"It's *boy band*, dumbass. Girl band isn't a thing."

Wolfgang sighed and leaned his head back. "Whatever you call this female power trip, my point—"

"Squad," Lucy said. "Girls call it a squad."

Wolfgang smirked, but his expression melted like ice on a griddle as the three women stared him down.

"Squad," he said. "Right. Squad, then. I really don't care. You can all get your feminine vengeance on Reed, but before you do, I *need* to talk to him."

"About *what*?" Banks's voice was barely above a hiss, her lips only inches from his face.

Wolfgang shook his head.

"Trust me, you wouldn't understand."

A soft snort erupted from all three women in unison, and Banks straightened, folding her arms. "Oh, we *wouldn't understand*?"

Wolfgang held up his palms, his wrists still taped to the chair. "It's not a gender thing. It's just science, okay? Advanced science. I spent years studying in some of the best schools—"

"You know, I don't like his tone," Banks said, still facing Wolfgang.

"Neither do I," Kelly growled.

Lucy stepped next to Banks and folded her arms. "He's saucy, isn't he? Completely unsexist in the midst of his *mansplaining*."

"Mansplaining?" Wolfgang laughed. "No, no. What I meant was—"

"Oh, now he's going to *clarify*." Banks rolled her eyes to the ceiling. "I've had about enough of this. Maybe it's time we clarified *our* position."

"Agreed." Kelly walked to the kitchen while Lucy and Banks circled behind the chair and began to tilt it back.

"Hey! I'm not a sexist. You misunderstood me!" Wolfgang wiggled in the chair, jerking his wrists and ankles in vain against the taped restraints. The back of the chair smacked against the floor, leaving him lying on his back with his legs suspended into the air.

Kelly returned from the kitchen, a pair of scissors in one hand and a wax candle in the other. Lucy produced a lighter from her pocket and lit the candle while Banks accepted the scissors and took a step toward Wolfgang's exposed crotch.

"Hey!" Wolfgang thrashed in the chair, his eyes growing wide. "What the hell? Look, I'm sorry. Women rule! You guys are sexy and smart and whatever!"

"And whatever?" Banks wrinkled her nose. "I'm not convinced."

She lowered the scissors against Wolfgang's knee, and with two quick snips, opened a long gash along the inside of his pants leg, exposing a milky white thigh.

"Whoa! Sister, let's put down the scissors, okay? Let's talk about this!"

"We *were* talking," Kelly snapped. "You had nothing to say, remember?"

Banks held out her hand. "Candle!"

Lucy's eyes flashed with delight as she passed the burning candle to Banks. A pool of molten wax swam around the base of the wick.

"Now, then," Banks said. "I'm going to ask again. Why do you want to talk to Reed?"

Wolfgang's brows pinched together, and his gaze flashed between the three women leaning over him. Kelly's face remained cold, and humor flashed across Lucy's eyes, but she made no move to save him.

He turned to Banks and grimaced.

"Look, I'd tell you if I could. It's just not—"

Banks cut him off. "Something I'd understand? I get it!"

She tipped the candle over, spilling a stream of liquid wax through the slice in his pants leg. It ran down his thigh toward his crotch, scalding and slowly drying along the way.

Wolfgang opened his mouth in a muted howl.

"Holy turkey mother stuffer!"

Kelly's face twisted into a disgusted glare. "What the hell? Are you five?"

"I don't curse," Wolfgang panted, beads of sweat dripping down his face.

"Well, shit," Banks said. "I must not be trying hard enough. Are there any more candles, Kelly?"

Kelly grinned for the first time. "Oh, yes. And some lighter fluid."

"Lighter fluid?" Banks said. "We could have a barbecue! Go get it."

Wolfgang whipped against the chair, banging his head against the floor as his skin turned a sickly shade of red beneath the pants. "Okay, you miserable, twisted freaks! Get me some ice. I'll talk."

"Ice?" Banks asked, a smirk playing across her lips. "Did he ask me for ice?"

"I think he asked you to ice his crotch," Lucy said.

Both women laughed, and the candle twitched, spilling more wax through the cut in Wolfgang's pants. He screamed, and Banks jerked the candle back, a momentary flash of guilt passing across her features.

She blew out the flame and nodded to Lucy.

"Okay. Let's pick him up."

They circled the chair and lifted Wolfgang by the shoulders, slamming the chair back down on all four legs.

Wolfgang spat on the floor, his upper lip trembling.

"Ice," he growled.

Banks leaned down until she was eye level with him. "Start talking."

Wolfgang's previous mood of satirical humor had vaporized. "*Ice*, you crazy witch. Then, I'll talk."

Lucy gave Banks's shoulder a gentle squeeze. "Give him the ice, sweetie."

Banks retreated to the kitchen, returning a moment later with a sandwich bag full of ice cubes. She dropped it between Wolfgang's thighs without ceremony, and he squeezed his legs together.

"Oh, sweet Moses," Wolfgang breathed. "That feels amazing."

A ripple of devilish laughter erupted from the room, and Banks stepped forward, pinching Wolfgang's ear and hauling his face toward hers.

"Okay, you bastard. Start talking, or Kelly's getting the lighter fluid."

16

Baton Rouge, Louisiana

Reed had never seen a state capitol building quite like Louisiana's. It wasn't made of marble, and it didn't consist of polished columns supporting a Washington-style dome. The bottom of the structure was built of limestone, forming a block building with narrow window slits. Rising out of the middle of that block foundation was a tower at least four hundred feet high, reaching toward the blackness of the Louisiana night sky.

He wasn't sure if the tower reminded him more of a 1930s office building or the futuristic seat of power for an authoritarian government. It was certainly beautiful, but something about it was impending. Threatening.

Or maybe it was just his own emotional reservations about the government after spending years living so far outside the law.

Reed left the BMW parked a few blocks away, lost amid a collection of black government sedans, and wandered into the park just south of the Capitol. The Mighty Mississippi River rolled slowly by on his left, while a small lake lay under the shadow of the tall building on the north side. The streets were wide, quiet, and empty, with only an occasional city cop rolling by amid the shadows.

Reed had been casing the Capitol for almost three hours, but it only

took him a few minutes to identify which floor Governor Maggie Trousdale's office was on. Google provided the answer to that. A momentary
review of Trousdale's Twitter feed produced a photo taken from her office
window, disclosing that it faced the Capitol steps and the lake on the north
side of the tower.

Reed couldn't see that angle of the building from where he sat parked
in the shadows two blocks away. So, by midnight, he made the decision to
step out of the shadows and close in on the Capitol. It was a risky move—
any number of surveillance devices, cops, or security personnel might
detect him.

But then again, this was downtown Baton Rouge. It was quiet and
peaceful. The center of government for the state. Was it all that unnatural
for a private citizen to take a walk next to the lake?

Reed had no idea. He wasn't sure what normal, private citizens did. But
the walk seemed like a milder risk than forgoing reconnaissance altogether,
so he circled the base of the Capitol and headed toward the lake without
looking back.

It was warm enough in Louisiana that he would've been comfortable in
a T-shirt, even though it was now late November, but Reed wore a light
jacket to conceal the SIG and the two extra magazines.

Five minutes of fast walking brought him fifty yards from the Capitol
steps, where a row of park benches stood back-to-back, some facing the
lake, while others faced the Capitol. Reed took a seat with his back to the
lake, situated under the shadows of an old oak tree with gnarled limbs that
twisted and curved up to the sky and down to the water.

The tree was likely here before the Capitol, Reed thought, and maybe
even before Louisiana was a state. Maybe this tree was planted by French
settlers or Native Americans, or maybe it predated both and survived
them all.

Things like the tree made Reed wonder if humanity was the problem
with the world. Nature simply existed, all at once, in all of its natural
turmoil and violence. Storms and ice ages came and went, trees grew and
fell, and animals hibernated and ate each other. Yet, despite the brutality of
it all, there was a sense of harmony. A sense of purpose. This was the way it

was and the way it was meant to be. There was a system—an established order.

Not so with people. People were always reinventing themselves and changing the rules. What was socially acceptable one century was perverse and offensive the next. People like Reed, who lived outside the law and made a way for themselves by whatever means necessary, were villains in the modern, enlightened era. But five hundred years ago? Reed could've been a warlord, a sort of god revered by the people.

Or maybe he would have been a rambling thug carrying a sword instead of a SIG. He didn't know, but it made him wonder if everybody was just fooling themselves, believing in peace and harmony and education, while this tree, this mighty oak, just outlasted them all in quiet splendor.

Reed leaned into the bench and traced the outline of the Capitol, working his way up one floor at a time until he settled on what he knew to be Maggie Trousdale's executive office. Even though most of the building was dark, a light was on behind her window, and he could see the faint outline of a slim, shapely figure walking back and forth behind the glass. Her long hair was tousled and tangled over her shoulders, but at almost a hundred yards distance, it was difficult to make out any more detail.

Reed reached beneath his jacket and withdrew the rifle scope. The dustcovers were already flipped open, and after a glance around to make sure nobody was watching, he lifted the optic while keeping both eyes open, staying alert for peripheral threats.

The crosshairs hovered over the executive office, and the woman came into view. She wore a simple white blouse that was as wrinkled and disheveled as her blonde hair, almost as though she'd just had a romp in the hay. But when she turned toward the window, the stress lines in her face removed any suspicion of recent ecstasy.

Maggie Trousdale was on the brink of a mental breakdown. He saw it in her stooped posture and slumped shoulders and the dark circles that broke through her smudged makeup. Maggie leaned against the windowsill and looked out toward the lake, staring directly over Reed's head, oblivious to his presence.

Reed zoomed the scope in a notch, holding it steady with his elbows pinned

against his ribcage for support. Maggie closed her eyes, and he saw her lip tremble. She lifted a tumbler into view and took a long gulp of an amber liquid,
swallowing and setting the glass on the windowsill without opening her eyes.

So, she was drunk. And distressed. And battered. What the hell was
going on?

Maggie stared out the window a moment more, then flinched and
turned away. Her back stiffened, and she ran a hand hastily through her
hair before walking out of sight.

Somebody must've walked in. Reed lowered the scope and checked his
watch. It was now approaching one a.m. Who else would be there at this
hour?

He tapped the scope against his knee and reviewed his mental notes
about Trousdale. She was in her early thirties, elected to her first term as
governor, had a bachelor's degree in pre-law from LSU, but never attended
law school. Her last job before being elected governor was on her family's
alligator farm—whatever an alligator farm was.

She launched her campaign for governor on Facebook only four
months before the election, and it quickly went viral, though it seemed like
she wasn't expecting to win or even gain traction. She ran on an agenda
about crime and deep-seated corruption in Baton Rouge, which resonated
with Louisianans. Even though Maggie was running as an Independent,
and both the Democrats and the Republicans had already nominated their
candidates and were pumping millions of dollars into their respective
campaigns, Maggie's grassroots platform exploded out of control after she
dominated a three-way debate. Eight weeks later, she defeated both contes-
tants by a comfortable margin.

Her supporters called her "Muddy Maggie" and were proud to remind
each other that she was "one of them." A swamp girl. A backwoods, home-
loving hero. Not a politician or a millionaire business owner or even a
highly-educated pundit. Just a gator farmer with a job to do.

And now here she was, in the governor's suite, drunk and strained, with
no idea that a killer sat a hundred yards away watching through a scope.

Reed replaced the optic in his coat and folded his arms. *Why does
Gambit want you dead, Muddy Maggie?*

It was the wrong question. That same curiosity had been the detriment to his life over the past few weeks. Hadn't he asked himself why these people wanted Mitchell Holiday dead? Hadn't that very question set off a chain reaction that led to this very predicament?

No, it was more complex than that. He was here because Oliver Enfield was a lying, backstabbing son of a bitch. He was here because Gambit held his father locked down with a gun to his head. He was here because he had a job to do, and it was reasonable to want to know why.

If Maggie was everything they said—a corruption-fighting idealist with a score to settle—what did that say about Aiden Phillips, Gambit's boss, the man who wanted her dead?

It said that he was probably at the heart of the corruption Maggie was fighting. He was probably the villain hiding in the shadows, waging war on the highest office of Louisiana.

Reed gritted his teeth and zipped his jacket. The thought-train was logical. The pieces fit together. Whatever sordid, messy operation Gambit and Aiden were involved in, it was headquartered, or at least operated within, Louisiana. Maggie had become a threat to it, just like Mitchell Holiday, Frank Morccelli, and David Montgomery had been. And just like Mitch and Frank and David, Aiden was coming for Maggie. Reed was just the middle man. The grunt.

A buzz erupted in his pocket. It was the phone Gambit had given him— his personal leash. Reed thought about letting it go to voicemail, just to yank Gambit around a little, but there was really no point in that. For all he knew, Gambit might actually have something useful to say.

Reed hit the answer button without speaking.

"Where are you?" Gambit's tone was demanding, and it pissed Reed off.

"Where I need to be."

A moment of silence.

Gambit must be deciding whether to react or ignore.

He chose to ignore.

"Are you making progress?"

"Yes."

"When do you expect to make a move?"

"When I'm ready."

The breath whistled between Gambit's clenched teeth. "Listen here, my friend. I don't have to remind you what's at stake. If you want to conclude our dealings in a mutually beneficial way, I suggest you remain cooperative."

Reed stood up and started back to the BMW. "You have a suggestion?"

A pause. Then Gambit cleared his throat. "Trousdale is holding a press conference in New Orleans, tomorrow. Lots of tall buildings around for you to shoot from. I thought you'd want to know."

Reed pondered the information for a moment. He already knew about the press conference, and he already knew his next play. He was more interested in why Gambit was calling. Was it because he wanted to check in, as he claimed, or was he calling to be sure Reed was at the press conference?

Reed gritted his teeth. He knew the answer. Gambit wanted a public execution. The purpose of the phone call was to find out Reed's plan—to set Reed up and make sure the cops or the FBI, or whoever, caught Reed immediately after Trousdale bit the dust, thereby killing two birds with one stone for Gambit.

It was the same shitty plan Oliver tried in Atlanta with the Holiday kill. Set up your best killer to get rid of your worst enemy, then tip off the cops. A nice, clean job with no loose ends.

Well, Reed saw that coming a mile away, but there was no need to tip his hand.

"I know about the press conference," he said. "I'm already making arrangements."

"As long as it gets done." Gambit played coy, but Reed wasn't fooled. He could hear the masked relief in Gambit's voice.

"It will. I'll check in with you tomorrow night after the dust settles. You better have my father ready, and he better not be harmed."

This time, the sly pleasure in Gambit's voice was barely concealed. "But of course, Reed. I wouldn't dream of hurting David. Talk soon."

The phone clicked off, and Reed shoved it into his pocket before ducking into the BMW. So the press conference was a setup. That was no surprise, but he wasn't yet in a position to throat-punch Gambit and rescue his father, so he would play along.

For now.

17

Wolfgang remained tied to the chair, his cheeks flushed from the pain of the wax burns on his thigh, but his voice was calm and measured. "Are you familiar with the disease cystic fibrosis?"

The three women sat around him, arms folded, faces impassive.

"Of course," Banks said. "Who isn't?"

"Lots of people, actually," Wolfgang said. "Which is why it isn't getting the attention or research dollars it deserves, despite the fact that it destroys a person's whole quality of life. CF breaks down a patient's lung capacity, deteriorating their ability to process oxygen, while it erodes their general health and compromises their immunity. It's a really nasty disease."

Banks grunted. "I'm somewhat familiar with chronic illness."

Wolfgang nodded somberly, and a momentary softness passed across his eyes. "Lyme's, right? I'm sorry."

Banks's back stiffened. She didn't expect Wolfgang to know, and she wasn't sure how he did. It didn't matter, though. There were more pressing issues at hand.

"Get to the point."

Wolfgang cleared his throat. "I have a doctorate in medical research from Edinburgh University. Over the past several years, I've been laboring to find a cure for CF, or at least a better treatment. It's a complex genetic science with lots of promising leads but very few actual developments. One hopeful study involves a gene therapy treatment that was developed for a disease called X-Linked, hypohidrotic ectodermal dysplasia, or XHLED. Basically, the treatment—"

Kelly broke in, her distorted lip curled in impatience. "What does any of this have to do with Reed?"

Wolfgang sighed. "I'm getting to that."

Banks placed a gentle hand on Kelly's arm and then jerked her head at Wolfgang, and he continued.

"XHLED is a disease that impacts babies prior to birth. It's genetic. Researchers have found a way to implement a protein replacement therapy which actually reverses the disease *prior to birth*. The project is still in development, but the results are promising. My hope is that these protein therapy methods could also be implemented to treat CF before birth and through adulthood. For the past several years, I've been experimenting with different protein therapy treatments, looking for a cure."

"Between killing people," Banks said.

Wolfgang shrugged. "I have no qualms bartering the blood of bad people for the hope of good ones. Life is an economy."

"We're not here to debate morality," Lucy said. "We want to know what your"—she made air quotes—"'research' has to do with Reed. Or any of us."

Wolfgang nodded. "Like I mentioned, the research is promising, but there have been no actual developments. Not yet. All the protein formulas I've experimented with have failed."

"So?" Lucy demanded. "You think Reed has the secret formula?"

"Actually, yes, I do."

The three women exchanged glances.

Banks leaned forward. "Why?"

"A few days ago, a parcel was left at my door with only two things inside —a note and a vile of liquid. After extensive testing of the liquid, I determined it to be some sort of protein-based formula, a DNA modifier."

"DNA modifier?" Lucy raised her eyebrows. "What the hell is that?"

"I'm not sure. I can't explain it. It's similar to the protein replacement therapy used by XHLED, but much more powerful. I tested it on some DNA sets that were damaged by pervasive CF and . . ."

"And what?" Banks prompted.

Wolfgang sighed, then shrugged. "And within forty-eight hours, the therapy stalled the growth of CF. Healthy DNA replication occurred."

The room was still, the quiet broken only by the distant snores of Baxter from the bedroom.

Kelly laughed.

"Okay, so what is this, some kind of superhero shit?"

Wolfgang glared. "It's nothing like that. I'm not even sure it's medicinal or safe. I just know that it changed the composition of the DNA. It stalled the CF and promoted the growth of healthy protein links."

"And you think this formula, whatever it is, could be used to cure CF?" Lucy asked.

"I don't know. I hope so. I'd need a few hundred hours of research time to even begin to answer that question. I have a lot of questions, but before I can begin, I need more of the formula."

"And you think Reed has it?" Banks asked. "Why?"

"I told you there was a note attached to the parcel. It said, '*Found what you are looking for. RM has the rest.*'"

Banks tightened her fingers around her arms and forced herself to remain calm.

"That's it? You got a creepy note from an unknown mailman that references *RM*, and you think that means Reed Montgomery?"

Wolfgang tapped a finger against the chair's arm. "I really don't know. I checked my cameras and found the images of the person who left the parcel. The person was small and stiff, like they were walking on a bad knee or something, and they were wrapped up in a jacket with a ski mask. They slipped right up to the door and didn't trigger my alarm until they were on their way out. It definitely wasn't Reed." Wolfgang jabbed his chin toward Lucy. "They were about your size, actually."

There was no accusation in his voice, but the implication was clear.

"You think I left a goodie bag on your porch?" Lucy laughed. "Sorry, bro. I don't even know where you live."

"Nobody does," Wolfgang said. "Which makes this even more troubling."

"Why do you think RM means Reed?" Kelly asked. "RM could be anybody."

"Absolutely. But whoever left the note intended for me to know who RM was. They didn't want to spell out the name, for whatever reason, and they also didn't think they needed to. They trusted me to know, and Reed is the first person who came to mind."

"So, he has this protein stuff?" Banks asked.

"Maybe," Wolfgang said. "Or maybe he knows who does or where it is. Maybe it has something to do with this war he's caught up in. I don't know. Like I told you, all I have right now are a bunch of questions. Has Reed ever mentioned medical stuff like this?"

Everybody looked at Banks, and she screwed her eyes shut, reviewing the last week in her mind. It was all a muddle, from the moment she saw Reed in the alley in Nashville to the moment he disappeared into the woods outside that prison, just a few nights prior.

"I don't remember," she said. "I don't think so."

"What were you doing at the prison?" Wolfgang asked.

Banks started to answer, but then she stopped. "You said you found Reed's phone at the prison. How did you even know to look there?"

The irritation started to slip through Wolfgang's practiced calm. "I saw a headline about David Montgomery escaping prison. It wasn't much of a leap to assume Reed was involved, so I decided to check out the premises. That's when I found the phone. It was clearly a burner, but I was able to backtrack it to this Hispanic guy in Mississippi—"

"T-Rex," Banks said. "You said that already."

"I'd heard of him before but never used him. Word on the street is that he's a little sloppy and loose-lipped, which turned out to be true. After a couple hundred bucks and the threat of a broken pelvis, he told me he sold two phones to Reed, and he gave me the numbers for each. I traced the second number and found you here."

Banks shot Lucy a sideways look, and Lucy offered a little shrug, as if to say, "*Yeah, he's good.*"

Banks turned back to Wolfgang. "So you came here, locked and loaded, to find Reed."

"Yes. Given our recent interactions, I thought he might be jumpy, so I was prepared. I had no intention of threatening him, though. I just want information. Whatever he knows."

"Right...." Banks stared at the floor and bit her lip.

"But," Wolfgang said, "he's not here, and you don't know where he is. So now that we've had this wonderful powwow, and all made some memories, it would be *terrific* if you cut me loose and let me get back to my research."

Kelly snorted. "No way, dude. We're not letting you back in our blind spot."

Wolfgang lifted an eyebrow. "So, what, you're gonna kill me and bury me in the woods?"

Kelly shrugged. "Works for me."

"Nobody is burying anybody in the woods," Banks said with a tired wave of her hand. "We've got work to do . . . all of us."

Lucy tilted her head, her mouth lifted in an inquisitive smile. "*We?*"

"Yes, we. You're all here for your own reasons, but we all need to find Reed." Banks nodded at Kelly. "You want to kill him. Lucy, you want to stop her from killing him. Wolfgang, you say he has this magic potion stuff. I don't care about any of that. I just want to find him because he owes me answers, and because I still want the head of the man who killed my father. But the fact is, I'm no whiz at tracking people or dealing with the sorts of criminals you guys deal with. So I need your help."

There was clear suspicion in everyone's eyes, marked with a noticeable hostility in Kelly's posture, but nobody immediately objected.

"Wolfgang, you tell a nice story," Banks said, "but if you ever try to blow me up again, I swear to god I'm going to let Lucy carve you in half."

Wolfgang glanced at Lucy, and his face turned a darker shade of red when she flashed him a toothy smile.

Banks turned to Kelly.

"I have a lot of sympathy for your situation, and I want to help you, but you've got to chill out. If you keep blowing up at everything, you're going to be left behind."

Kelly grunted and stared at the floor.

Banks ran both hands through her hair. "Can the two of you cooperate long enough to find Reed?"

Wolfgang and Kelly nodded.

Lucy touched Banks on the arm.

"Sweetie, I don't think this is a good idea."

"Yeah, well, nobody asked you. I appreciate you taking care of me and all, but you're the only one here who isn't directly interested in finding Reed. So, you do whatever. We're going."

Lucy removed her hand and tapped her leg for a moment, then nodded. "Fair enough."

Banks gestured toward Wolfgang. "Untie him. He'll behave."

Lucy stared Wolfgang down, then stepped across the room and sliced away the tape with a pocket knife.

Wolfgang rubbed his wrists and rolled his head back.

"Oh, thank heavens. I've got to pee so bad."

Lucy leaned down, placing one delicate hand on Wolfgang's scalded thigh, before whispering in his ear.

Banks couldn't hear the words, but by the pallor that passed across Wolfgang's face, she knew they constituted a threat.

Wolfgang laughed and nodded, and Lucy stepped back.

"All right, then," she said. "We're gonna find Reed. How the hell do we do that?"

Banks smiled, feeling a soft gleam of hope ignite in her tired mind. "Actually . . . I have an idea."

18

Baton Rouge, Louisiana

The hotel was dark and musty, much like every ratty hotel Reed had ever stayed in. That was the downside of traveling incognito—the only hotels that let you check in with cash and without an ID were the bad ones. But he was used to it. An old, lumpy bed with sour sheets under a ceiling speckled with mold was about as good as he could expect only miles from the swamps of south Louisiana. At least it was quiet and isolated.

Reed sat on the edge of the bed, his right ankle propped up on his left knee. His pants leg was pulled up to expose the nylon strap of the ankle monitor. The tiny black unit featured a single red light that flashed every five seconds.

Reed ran his finger along the inside of the strap, feeling for the metallic band encased inside the nylon. The band was probably made of copper or steel, something conductive that completed a circuit from one side of the monitor to the other, ensuring that if the strap were cut and the strip severed, the circuit would be broken and an alert would be triggered.

It was an impossible problem. The only way to remove the monitor would be to break the circuit, regardless of whether the monitor was cut off or removed with the actual key that unlocked the strap. Either way, the monitor would send a signal to whatever computer it was connected to, logging the event, and then Reed would be screwed.

Reed twisted on the bed and lifted a small plastic bag off the pillow. It was full of odds and ends he had picked up the previous day at an electronics store—a small spool of copper wire, some solder, a soldering iron, and a pair of insulated cutting pliers.

He plugged the soldering iron into a nearby outlet before setting it on the nightstand and picking up the pliers. There was really no way to ensure that this would work. Reed's knowledge of electronics was somewhat rudimentary, but then again, the basic concept of an ankle monitor wasn't exactly rocket science. It was a GPS unit designed to track him and issue an alert if the circuit surrounding his leg was broken, so the key to removing it without triggering the alert would be to ensure that the circuit was never broken or grounded.

Reed grabbed the pliers by their insulated handles, ensuring that his skin never came in contact with the metal. He wasn't sure if touching the metal band beneath the nylon would trigger the alert, but it might. Better to be safe.

The pliers sliced through the nylon with relative ease, and after thirty seconds of effort, Reed exposed the band.

It was copper, just as he suspected, and not particularly strong, but highly conductive, ensuring that any interruption in the circuit would be detected.

The soldering iron was hot on the nightstand. Reed unspooled twelve inches of the wire and stripped away the end of the plastic insulation with the pliers, then gently touched the tip to the exposed copper band and paused.

Nothing happened. At least, nothing noticeable.

The red light continued to blink every five seconds. Reed exhaled a breath he didn't know he was holding and picked up the soldering iron. It took only a few seconds to solder the wire to the band, ensuring a secure and conductive bond between the two. Reed rotated the monitor 180 degrees and made a similar cut on the other side of the nylon strap before repeating the procedure with the other end of the wire. In less than ten minutes, the operation was complete, and he sat back to regard his handiwork.

The circuit was now secure, with electrical current flowing from the monitor into both the copper band and the wire, theoretically ensuring that if either the wire or the band were cut, the other would assume the full load of the current and prevent the circuit from breaking.

It made sense, logically, like diverting the flow of water from a pipe before cutting into the pipe. At face value, it *should* work.

Reed sighed and picked up the pliers. There was only one way to find out. His entire plan hinged on being able to ditch the monitor.

A few quick cuts tore away the nylon in the middle of the band. Reed paused a moment longer, ensured his hands weren't touching the metal part of the pliers, then bit his lip and cut through the band.

For an agonizing four seconds, he waited for the red light to blink and then for the phone in his pocket to ring. He waited for Gambit's goons to kick the door open and rush in.

The red light blinked. Reed exhaled again, his shoulders dropped, and he laid down the pliers. Another ten seconds passed, and the red light blinked twice, five seconds apart. Reed gently grabbed the severed ends of the nylon strap and pulled them away from his leg. The twelve inches of wire provided sufficient wiggle room for him to pull the entire apparatus over his ankle and around his foot.

And then he was free.

He set the device on the bed and watched it for a minute longer, counting twelve separate flashes of the red light. Nothing had changed, and as far as he could tell, the current from the monitor continued to flow through the copper wire, unobstructed by the severed copper band.

Reed rubbed his ankle. It felt damn good to have the monitor gone, like taking off a rucksack after a long march. He placed the monitor gently inside the plastic bag from the electronics store and wrapped it up. The bag would provide some minor protection from any disturbances that could trigger the alarm, but he would still need to be careful. Anything could happen.

He stood up and stretched, then rotated and looked down at the bed. Lying there in a neat pile were several small boxes, all labeled in tiny black letters that formed Spanish words, and on the corner of one box, Reed saw the insignia of the Mexican Army.

T-Rex had arrived only hours before to deliver the pricey cargo: ten pounds of C4.

19

"Of all the vile habits, God hates the bottle the most!"

Maggie could still imagine her deceased grandmother sitting in her armchair, a copy of the *Times-Picayune* folded over one thigh, and her outstretched finger wagging in the air. "Of all the vile habits, God hates the bottle the most!"

It was an odd sentiment for anybody living so close to Bourbon Street to hold, but then, Margery Trousdale, Maggie's namesake, wasn't from Louisiana. She was from old South Georgia, deep in the heart of peanut fields connected by quiet dirt roads, where the Southern Baptist Church—not the Roman Catholic Church—presided over the religious affections of society.

And to a Southern Baptist, murder itself was not so great a crime as a sip of whiskey.

Imagine if she saw me now, Maggie thought. She tipped her glass back and drained the last drops of Johnny Walker from its bottom. They tasted stale in her mouth, either because she'd been staring at the glass for the better part of an hour, or because she'd already consumed four glasses.

Margery Trousdale would be soul-crushed, Maggie knew. The old woman was no fool. She knew her family and even her Catholic husband was no stranger to the bottle, but she didn't lecture them out of anger. To Granny Marge, her passionate lectures were an expression of tough love. She would turn a blind eye to the occasional case of beer at a gator grilling party, but if she had ever seen her drunken granddaughter slouched over the executive desk of the highest office of the state, well . . . it was a good thing she had already passed on because that would've done her in.

Maggie fumbled for the bottle and dumped the last few swallows into the glass. The room around her was quiet, darkened by the fall of night around the old city.

Coulier had gone back to Texas, claiming he had some urgent family matter to attend to, but Maggie had never heard him mention a family before. He probably just wanted to slip away quietly before the fallout, and she'd probably receive a signed copy of his resignation in the mail before the end of the week and never see him again.

Could she blame him? She wanted to. Dammit, she wanted to. It was Coulier's idea to rig the closure of the port and launch into the mad, desperate attempt to track down an invisible criminal syndicate headed by the shadowy man known only as *Gambit*. Wasn't it Coulier's idea to board that ship, the *Santa* something? Wasn't it Coulier's assumption that Gambit's operation would orbit around the Port of New Orleans in the first place?

It was certainly Coulier's idea to frame Dan Sharp for the entire mess, and did he frame him for the death of Attorney General Matthews?

She didn't think so. As sloppy, destructive, and unhelpful as Coulier had been, what possible motive could he have for sabotaging Sharp to that degree?

None of this was Coulier's fault. She wanted to blame him and call the news and spill her guts and pin everything on his shoulders, but she couldn't. As many times as she reached for the phone, she always stopped. Another overused adage from her grandmother rang in her ears every time, as loud and sharp as if the old woman were sitting next to her:

"A leader is responsible."

Maggie closed her eyes and rested her forehead against the damp lip of the glass. Margery Trousdale was always ranting about leadership, always fussing about failed politicians and executives and community leaders. To her credit, she didn't just rant, she took action whenever possible, leading projects and campaigning for better leaders.

Maybe it was Granny Marge who inspired Maggie to run for office, to make a change, to challenge the status quo. If so, it was ironic because Margery Trousdale would have shit a brick at the thought of a female governor.

Maggie smiled longingly at that thought. What she wouldn't give to see her old Granny again. She would tell her absolutely everything—every sordid detail and poor decision—and she'd ask her what a true leader would do and what a wise governor who loved her state more than life itself would say. Would she resign? Would she admit to everything?

Or would she stay in the fight?

The phone rang on her desk, dull and distant. She blinked back the intoxication and let it ring three more times before reluctantly lifting it to her ear.

"Governor Trousdale." She instantly kicked herself for answering the phone with slurred words. What if this were the press or an investigator?

"Maggie?"

The familiar Cajun warble of her mother rang over the phone, and Maggie felt a wave of relief wash through her.

"Mama, it's me."

"Oh, god, Maggie. I've been calling all over for you. You still in the city?"

For her mother, any place other than the swamps was "*the city.*" In a further twist of irony, Maggie's entire family held greater suspicion of danger in the city than they did for the gator and snake-filled swamps they called home.

"Yes, Mama. I'm still at the Capitol."

"You should come home. You need to eat. I've got a big kettle of gumbo. Your brother went out today and caught some shrimp. You need to eat, Maggie."

"I'm not hungry, Mama."

"Is that Maggie?" She heard the gruff, grizzled voice of her father, then the phone clicked as it was switched to speaker.

"Hey, Daddy," Maggie mumbled. The phone clattered around as her father held it up to his ear. He had no idea how a speakerphone worked.

"Maggie? They been talkin' about you on the news again. That smug son of a bitch on the Foxes channel. I'm about to send your brother down there to kick some ass."

Maggie couldn't resist a smile. "No, Daddy. He's just a journalist doing his job."

"Well, he's got a mighty smart mouf. Says all kinda long, fancy words I never heard of. Sumptin' about conspiracy and corruption."

Maggie leaned back in her chair and blinked back tears.

"Yeah, Daddy. I know."

Another rustling sound of plastic against cloth, then the calm drawl of her little brother's voice rang over the phone.

"Hey, sis, it's Larry. You're off speaker. You okay?" Larry was better educated than his parents but still maintained the same simple soul.

Maggie wiped her eyes. "Yeah, bro. All good. Just got some stuff to figure out."

"I saw the news. They're saying some stuff about Uncle Dan. Something about murder."

"It's not true. I'm taking care of it."

"Okay, I knew it wasn't. Uncle Dan wouldn't hurt a swamp rat. But really, you should come home for a bit and clear your head. You can't get work done on whiskey alone."

That was Larry, wise beyond his years. Calm and perceptive. And so trusting.

"I hear you, Larry. Can you put me back on speaker?"

Another rustle, then the phone beeped.

"We're all here, sweetie," her mother said.

Maggie swallowed and closed her eyes. Every moment was mental torture, but she had to say it. It was the only right thing to do.

"Listen, I need to tell you all something. I'm going to New Orleans tomorrow. We're reopening the port."

"Maggie, that's wonderful!" Her mother's enthusiasm was unbounded. "I knew you'd get people back to work."

"'Bout damn time," her father grunted. "Folk got bills to pay!"

"Guys, please. I'm not finished." Maggie braced herself. "Tomorrow . . . well, I'm going to say some things on TV. Things that I have to say. Things that may be hard for you to hear. I just want you to know that I'm saying them because they're true, and I have to tell the truth. But I'm sorry . . . I'm so sorry."

The line was silent. The phone clicked off of speaker, and she heard her mother's soft breath. "Maggie? What are you talking about?"

"I love you," Maggie whispered. She hung up and slumped over her desk, her face falling into her hands. There was no holding back the tears now.

20

T-Rex was exhausted. It had been a bone-grinding sort of day, beginning at six in the morning in Memphis, when he started his van and drove six hours to Tyler, Texas, to pick up a new batch of cheap and dirty Mexican C4. He drove five more hours to Baton Rouge, where he delivered the C4 to The Prosecutor in an empty parking lot behind a grocery store. Reed was quiet and uninterested in discussing the blonde woman T-Rex had last seen him with, which was disappointing because T-Rex hadn't forgotten about her. He often found his thoughts drifting back to her gently swaying hips and sassy smile, or the glint in her eyes when she slapped him.

He wasn't going to lie about it; he liked it that way—rough and sassy. T-Rex made plenty of money, and women weren't difficult to come by, but that only made his exploits bland and easy. He liked a challenge. He longed for a true fireball like this blonde, all piss and vinegar, with all the right curves in all the right places.

As it turned out, the gods of desire and ecstasy smiled on him. T-Rex could hardly believe his luck when an unknown number rang through one of his burner phones, and he answered it to hear the smooth voice of the blonde on the other end.

Her name was Banks. Reed had abandoned her, she was lonely, and she had been thinking about him *all day long*.

T-Rex turned north out of Baton Rouge and crashed toward Mississippi like a bat out of hell, hardly containing his excitement. It took five hours to reach Tupelo, and his eyes stung with exhaustion by the time he finally rolled into the little city, but it was going to be worth it. He was sure of that. He imagined slow dancing with the blonde in the secluded hotel room she selected, wrapping his arms around her neck and kissing her, soft and slow. They would sip true Mexican tequila and find their way out of their clothes.

The van squeaked to a halt in the back of the motel parking lot, and T-Rex ran his tongue over the palm of his hand before slicking back his wavy black hair. Normally, he'd want to shower and put on something nice before meeting a lady, but perhaps she wasn't a lady, and she was just as easy as the others. She certainly sounded hot and heavy on the phone. Had he completely misjudged her?

Tomorrow he might call her as bland as the rest, but tonight he would make love to her the way only a suave gentleman from south of the border knew how.

Something clicked against the window, and T-Rex jumped. Banks stood just outside the van, her long hair hanging loose next to flushed cheeks. Her lips were lined with thick red lipstick, and she was dressed in a revealing black dress, the kind of thing suited to a cocktail party or a late-night rendezvous at a cheap hotel.

T-Rex recoiled for a moment at the sight of her nose. It was purple with bruises that traced their way beneath her eyes—altogether unpleasant to look at.

Then again, there was plenty else to look at. Had Reed beaten her? Was that why she called him?

That bastard.

T-Rex clicked the door open and slid out, deciding at once to ignore her nose and enjoy the rest.

"Oh, baby. You lookin' fine tonight!"

Banks smiled seductively, then placed a gentle kiss on his cheek, only half an inch from his ear. Her voice was soft and warm.

"Come on, baby. I've got a room ready for us."

T-Rex almost ran across the parking lot, holding her by one hand and tripping on the curb outside the first floor of rooms.

"Easy, baby," Banks murmured. "We've got all night."

She stepped ahead and led him down a hallway to the back of the hotel. Another row of doors waited over a dirty sidewalk, their frames painted in peeling orange paint. T-Rex slowed down and followed her to number 18. Banks slid a plastic key into the lock and pushed the door open, then stepped back, her hips swinging ever so slightly as she moved.

T-Rex felt his heart rate quicken, and he rushed forward, grabbing her by the hand. The two stumbled into the dark room, and the door shut behind them.

"The light switch is on the left-hand wall," Banks whispered. "Turn it on for me?"

T-Rex tripped and stumbled, feeling for the switch until he found it and flipped it on, flooding the room with light. He blinked as his vision adjusted, then his heart leapt into his throat.

A tall, slender man stood inches in front of him, his arms crossed and a smug smile covering his face. T-Rex recognized him immediately as the stranger from a few days prior—the man who wanted to know about the cell phones T-Rex sold Reed.

T-Rex blinked in confusion, and the man's smirk widened. Something moved in the shadows behind the man, and T-Rex saw a third figure—a woman, dressed head-to-toe in a black robe, with only her eyes visible.

T-Rex squealed and stepped back. "What the hell kind of party is this? Baby, I'm kinky but—"

His shoulder blades slammed into the wall, and T-Rex flinched as a razor-sharp blade brushed his shoulder and came to rest only a breath away from his throat. A short, petite woman with flaming-red hair pulled back into a ponytail stepped out of the shadows next to him, pivoting to his front while keeping the blade near his windpipe. She wore a skintight suit and had a sword strapped to her hip.

"Aw, man. What the *hell*?" T-Rex's face broke into a glare, and he glanced to his right.

Banks stood a few feet away, hands on her hips, smirking.

"Sorry, *baby*."

T-Rex snapped, "Is this a robbery? You want my stinkin' *money*, bro? This is sick! I drove all the way from . . . "

He trailed off, and his eyes narrowed as his gaze switched from one face to the next. He folded his arms.

"What do you want?"

The redhead smirked. "I want you in bed, on your back, all spread out and helpless."

His cheeks flushed. "What kind of sick show is this?"

The edge of the blade nicked his throat, and he felt a warm stream of blood running down his neck.

The man spoke for the first time. "I wouldn't upset her if I were you." He touched his own neck, and T-Rex saw a scab that looked like it may have been caused by the same blade.

"On the bed, now." The redhead motioned with her free hand, and T-Rex reluctantly lay on the bed, wiggling until he was centered over the comforter. The woman in the black robes stepped forward, a coil of light rope appearing from the folds of her clothing.

"Hey!" T-Rex started to sit up, but the blade pressed against his neck again, and he slumped back.

Banks approached him from the other side and helped the silent woman in the robes tie his hands to the bedposts, then they moved to his feet.

T-Rex's voice wavered on the edge of a sob. "Look, don't hurt me, okay? I got kids, man! And a wife. A mother. I've got a pet parrot, man!"

The redhead laughed. "Bullshit. All you've got is a big, sticky problem. You see, my friends and I have spent the last three hours discussing our favorite forms of bedroom perversion. We've come up with a pretty good list. I'm curious. Do you like lighter fluid? Because Kelly *loves it*."

The redhead motioned to the woman in the robes, who turned and faced T-Rex. Her dark eyes glinted through the slit in her face mask, sending a cold chill ripping through his body.

The ropes tightened around his ankles, restraining him to the bed. Banks and Kelly backed off, and the redhead hopped onto the bed with an agile jump that landed her small feet between his knees. She grinned down at him with a semi-devilish glint in her eyes as the tip of her blade danced down his neck, tracing his torso down to his belt buckle and then one inch lower.

"Now then, *baby* . . ." Banks said, stepping up beside him. "We've only got one question. *Where* is Reed Montgomery?"

21

Reed's shoes sank into the muddy shore on the south side of the Mississippi River. He shoved his hands into his pockets and squinted against the rising sun as he stared across the slow-moving river at the Port of New Orleans. The Crescent City Connection bridge shot across the water directly overhead, its rusty, red-metal framework glistening in the warmth of the morning and providing him only moderate relief from the brightness.

It was going to be a hot day. He wouldn't need the coat, which made disguising his person—not to mention his gun—an increasing challenge. Reed could already see state troopers and security personnel bustling on the other side of the river, setting up a podium for the governor's speech. There were dozens of cops, but to the trained eye, it wasn't an altogether efficient operation.

That was good. The mild chaos and inevitable tension between the state, city, and parish cops would offer Reed the perfect opening to slip inside their ranks and plant the bomb. It would be like walking into a darkened movie theater without a ticket. As long as he was quiet, nobody would stop him, but he'd need a better disguise than a thick coat on a hot morning. Something that would blend in, not stick out.

He turned away from the water and back toward the car. He knew exactly where to find it.

Reed correctly assumed that the Louisiana state troopers would perform fringe support for Governor Trousdale's primary security detail, and it took him less than fifteen minutes to identify a lone trooper at the edge of the crowd. The man was tall, broad, and generally representative of Reed's physique, which was all he needed.

He left Officer Rich Bordeaux unconscious and restrained in the basement of a bar, two blocks from the port. Bordeaux was a big man with a hat and uniform that fit Reed nicely. A quick tap to the base of his skull was all that was necessary to subdue him, and Reed left him a bottle of water and a couple aspirin to treat the headache when he woke up.

Reed straightened his tie and stepped back onto the street, the hat cocked on his head at the same angle Bordeaux had worn it. Troopers spent the majority of their days working alone, patrolling highways and parish roads, so he hoped that meant Bordeaux didn't actually know many of the people he'd be working with, and therefore nobody would notice the disconnect between Bordeaux's nameplate and Reed's face. There was no way to be sure.

Reed walked the two blocks back to the port and infiltrated the gathering crowd of media, curious citizens, and angry port workers encircling the podium.

Trousdale's security had done a good job of setting the place up. There was a bulletproof shield that stood ten feet high, twenty feet distant from the podium, ensuring that any random hothead who slipped through the checkpoints with a pistol wouldn't be able to crack off a lucky shot. The transportable podium stood eighteen inches off the ground and was covered with a black cloth embroidered with the state seal of Louisiana. A microphone, teleprompter, and a stand with a bottle of water all waited in the middle of the podium, while black-suited guards walked back and forth, making final checks and adjustments.

It would be perfect, Reed thought, and ideally suited to execute his plan without any collateral damage. He swept his gaze around the buildings that encircled the port and quickly identified all three snipers. There would be three, of course: one to keep a constant eye on the governor and track her position if she needed to be moved, and two more to keep seamless surveillance over the crowd while constantly searching for threats.

It was the first sniper keeping his eyes on the governor who would be the problem. In an ideal world, Reed would've found a way to disable him beforehand, but there wasn't enough time for that.

He checked his watch. It was twenty minutes until the governor's speech. Given the hostile nature of the crowd, he doubted she would appear before then.

Reed stepped out of the crowd and walked one block away from the port and around a corner. The BMW waited in a small pay-per-hour parking lot, its nose pointed outward toward the street. He hit the trunk release button on the key fob and ducked his head down, dragging out the duffle bag. Inside were two packages: one of them contained eight pounds of T-Rex's C4, while the other was packed with the remaining two pounds. Both were equipped with electronic detonators, wired and ready to go.

Reed walked back to the crowd, keeping the bag swinging by his side, his shoulders loose, and his face twisted into the sort of authoritative, some-what-aloof expression he imagined troopers used, though he wasn't actually sure.

Another trooper almost bumped into him as he passed but offered Reed nothing more than a brief nod before hurrying on. Forty yards farther, Reed circled the edge of the semi-circular bulletproof shield and stepped toward the podium.

"Hey! You there. Where are you going?"

Reed turned around. One of Trousdale's security detail, dressed in a black suit with a curly wire running toward his ear, held up a hand.

Reed stopped and cocked his head.

"What's in the bag?"

Reed unzipped the bag and pulled the flaps back.

"Water . . . for the press conference. You want some?"

The man seemed briefly confused, frowning down at the bag. There were nine bottles inside, six of them still wrapped in a plastic package, while the other three were loose.

Reed selected one of the loose bottles and tossed it to him.

"Here, better hydrate. It's warm today."

The agent caught it and offered a quick grin. "Hey, thanks. You can put those over there, I guess. Just get rid of the bag. They don't like them lying around."

"No problem."

The guy walked off, and Reed turned around, resisting the urge to glance up at the snipers. He had no doubt that at least two of them had viewed the exchange. He could only hope their concerns were suitably disarmed.

Approaching the podium, Reed scooped the six-pack of water bottles from the bag and bent over, setting it down at the back of the podium, just under its lip where the cloth parted. He then straightened, made a show of stretching his back, and circled the podium before depositing two more bottles in front of it, just inside the bulletproof shield.

This was the moment of truth. There was no real reason to leave bottles here. A close inspection of either bottle would reveal that their contents weren't liquid. But maybe, with some luck, everybody would be too busy and too distracted to question something so insignificant.

22

Hwy 45 South
Mississippi

"Reed's in Baton Rouge! I sold him ten pounds of C4 this morning."

As it turned out, T-Rex was no Fort Knox. He squealed only moments after being tied to the bed, and over the next ten minutes, the group mined as much information as they could out of him. Then, after promising to alert the front desk in a couple hours, they left him tied up and took inventory of his van on their way out.

The panel van, painted with gaudy images of Greek gods, was loaded to the gills with every sort of weaponry and combat equipment imaginable. Wolfgang said he was fully equipped, and Lucy seemed happy with her swords and knives, but Kelly and Banks dug through the boxes and trays and surfaced with enough firepower to continue their mini-war. Kelly selected a Smith & Wesson M&P 9mm compact, along with an extra magazine, a flashlight, and a holster. The weapon disappeared beneath her burka like a shadow.

Banks found a small revolver—another Smith & Wesson—chambered in .38 Special, and tucked it into her waistband. On her way out, she spotted a pump shotgun on a rack. It was short and black, with a pistol grip and sawed-off barrel. Upon further inspection, she found it to be chambered in 20-gauge, a lighter-recoiling load still fully capable of knocking a grown man off his feet. Banks was very familiar with shotguns—she had fired several of them while growing up in Mississippi. Something about the simple elegance of the sawed-off was attractive to her.

She found a bandolier of 20-gauge buckshot and grabbed the gun, piling out of the van and nodding to the others.

"I'm good. Let's roll."

Wolfgang's car was a Mercedes AMG S63 Coupe, and it was by far the nicest car Banks had ever ridden in. Lucy and Kelly, the two smallest members of what Lucy named "The Ass-Kicking Squad Plus This Dude," piled into the cramped back seats of the car while Banks dropped the shotgun into the trunk and slid into the front passenger seat. There had been a brief debate over whether to drive Lucy's rented SUV, but Wolfgang wouldn't hear of it.

"Style. Your squad needs it," he said as he hit the start button and the Mercedes' giant engine roared to life. That sound, coupled with the glowing Mercedes logo on the front grill, brought a twist to Banks's stomach. She remembered the last time she had seen this car, in another forest, on another road, in another state. She remembered the rattle of automatic gunshots as Wolfgang pressed a submachine gun through his window and opened fire on her Beetle.

She paused a moment, staring him down. The tall man dressed in a wool coat, with his hair neatly combed to one side and a wry smile on his face, seemed nothing like the cool, calculated killer who had launched grenades at her in North Carolina. She knew instinctively that she should be wary of this man. Maybe even afraid. But somehow, she wasn't. Maybe it was because Lucy sat directly behind him, one of her long knives lying across her lap. Or maybe it was because Banks had spoken to Wolfgang and understood him better.

Or maybe it was because she was stupid, she thought. Stupid, stupid, stupid. Hadn't she trusted Reed and almost anyone who asked her to her whole damn life? Hadn't that led her into this strange world of bloodshed?

Banks wiggled deeper into the plush seat of the Mercedes and closed her eyes, tracing her way back to the last moment she saw Reed as he disappeared into that Alabama forest. He had glanced over his shoulder, held her gaze for a moment, and she saw something in his eyes that she hadn't before—something soft, deep, and passionate.

It was longing, aching pain. And yet, there was more to it than that. There was something else, something mysterious that radiated from his very soul.

Banks had no idea what it was or what it meant, but she knew exactly how it made her feel. It made her feel like the whole world had fallen away, and nothing and nobody except the two of them remained. It made her feel like there was another man behind the cold-hearted face of the killer she knew—a man who was more complex, more conflicted, and maybe more good than she had first assumed.

I KNOW YOU SAID NOT TO SAY IT, BUT I LOVE YOU. GOODBYE.

Once more, Reed's last text message rang through her mind. The burner phone was still in her pocket, but she didn't need to review it to remember those words. She had read them a hundred times until they were burned into her memory forever.

Don't follow. I love you. I love you. I love you. Goodbye.

He said he loved her. Did he mean it? Did she believe it? Was this brutal, bloody man capable of love?

Wolfgang reached forward and flicked a switch on the dash. The car was flooded with the gentle melody of an opera streaming from speakers that probably cost more than Banks's Beetle.

"What bullshit is this?" Kelly snapped. She sat behind Banks, still wrapped in her burka.

"This, my dear woman, is *style*," Wolfgang said. "I don't expect you to understand."

"It sounds like a squealing pig. A squealing French pig."

"French pig?" The indignation on Wolfgang's face was absolute. "And what would *you* know about anything French?"

Kelly's eyes flashed behind the burka. "*C'est un beau pays, plein de souvenirs.*"

Everyone looked up, and Banks ratcheted her head around the seat. "You speak French? I had no idea. What does that mean?"

Kelly turned away, staring out of the small slit of a window next to her compact rear seat. "It means it is a beautiful country. Full of memories."

Banks nodded slowly. "I've never been. I would love to go."

Kelly snorted. "Maybe Reed will take you. That's where we met. On a beach, in a Ferrari, under the moon."

Kelly's tone grew increasingly sarcastic as she spoke, and an awkward stillness filled the car. Wolfgang and Lucy both avoided Banks's gaze. She twisted and settled back in the passenger seat, a knot forming in her stomach. Had Reed loved Kelly? She didn't know much about them, how they met, or what tore them apart. Reed's references to Kelly were few and far between, leaving almost no detail about their romance. She got the feeling they both cared about each other, but then something happened.

Maybe it was Reed and his ruthless lifestyle. What woman could live with that?

Only a woman who thought she could change him, Banks thought. Maybe Kelly had, but maybe Kelly had been proven wrong.

Wolfgang cleared his throat. "What kind of music *do* you like?"

Kelly said nothing for a moment, then grunted. "Lil Wayne."

Wolfgang frowned. "Little Wayne? Is that a band?"

A chuckle erupted from the women.

"You've *got* to be kidding me," Banks said. "You've never heard Lil Wayne?"

"No . . ."

Banks depressed the voice command on the dash and instructed Wolfgang's phone to play Lil Wayne's hits. "Uproar" came ripping through the speakers only a moment later, and Wolfgang's face twisted into a dark scowl.

"What in the world . . ."

Banks began to snap her fingers and swing her shoulders, and Lucy clapped. Even Kelly looked forward, the hint of a smile in her eyes.

"This is *not* music!" Wolfgang said.

"You're right," Banks said. "This is *art*."

Wolfgang reached for the stereo, but Banks slapped his hand away, and Lucy laughed. The two women began to rap along, barely keeping up with Lil Wayne's practiced rhythm, until Kelly joined in a moment later.

Wolfgang exhaled an abused sigh.

"I knew I was gonna regret this."

23

"Are you ready, Madam Governor?"

Maggie sat alone in the back seat of her SUV, staring through the window at nothing. The man who leaned in across the front seat was one of her security staff—a detail commander also conducting coordination activities in place of her chief of staff, Yolanda Flint. Yolanda resigned three days earlier in the fallout of Sharp being arrested. Maggie guessed she had a pretty good idea about what went down inside the administration. Yolanda knew everything, after all. It was part of her job.

Maggie didn't blame her for getting out before the fireworks started. It was the logical thing to do, the thing that Maggie herself longed to do. If only she could check out of this damn town and run away to the family home, deep in the swamps, and forget about Baton Rouge and the politics and the deception and all the bad, bad decisions she had made.

What business did she have being governor? She was barely more than a kid, inexperienced and full of too much passion and not enough discernment. She was a fool.

Maggie held back her tears. It was over now. She would go outside, step up onto that podium, and make it right. She'd admit to everything and probably be arrested, but at least Sharp would be cleared, and she could sleep with a clear conscience.

"Madam Governor?" The guard repeated from the front seat. "Are you ready, ma'am?"

Maggie looked up, meeting the man's gaze in her rearview mirror. It was Officer O'Dell, a member of her personal detail from the first day she took office. He was a quiet man, but there was a strength in his eyes that made her feel safe whenever he was around. Now that she faced him from the back seat, she wondered what his story was. His accent said local, but his posture and the wariness in his eyes said he had traveled far from home and seen things that had changed him. Was he an ex-soldier? Probably.

So he was an American hero, then. A public servant. Another good citizen that she had betrayed with her failed leadership.

Maggie looked down. "I'm ready," she mumbled.

The door of the SUV burst open, and Maggie flinched. Coulier appeared, dressed in an impeccable new suit, a confident glint in his eye.

"Coulier?" Maggie said, surprised. "What are you doing here?"

Coulier frowned, then he twitched his head toward O'Dell. "Give us a minute?"

O'Dell looked reluctant, but he nodded and slipped out of the SUV. Coulier piled into the back seat and shut the door, straightening his tie.

"What are you doing here?" Maggie asked again. "I thought you went back to Texas."

"I did. It was an urgent family matter, like I said. A death, actually. A great-aunt of mine. I flew back immediately after the funeral."

"But . . . why?" Maggie couldn't hide the emotion or confusion in her voice.

Coulier frowned again. "Because I'm the attorney general of Louisiana. I've got work to do."

"But, I thought . . ."

"Thought I was skipping town? I apologize. Family deaths really do come at the worst times. But I'm back now, ready to serve at your discretion. What next, Madam Governor?"

Maggie stared down at her clenched hands and then unclenched them.

"I have to resign. It's the only right thing. I have to clear Sharp's name. I know you're gonna try to talk me out of it, but—"

"No, I'm not going to question you any further, ma'am. Secretary Warner will make an . . . average governor, I suppose. Good enough until an election can be held."

Warner was Louisiana's secretary of state, and with the lieutenant governor unable to serve, Warner was next in line for the executive office.

Maggie nodded but didn't reply.

"Do you know why I took this job, Maggie?"

"Because you have a vendetta with some business people in New Orleans. You wanted revenge."

"Yes, I want revenge. And I'll get it, one way or the other. But that's not why I took the job."

"Okay. Why?"

"I took the job because there's one thing I hate in this world more than the devil himself. And that's bullies. People who get their way, regardless. I hate these people with a passion that is both dark and consuming. It's my life's mission to crush them. When I met you, I saw the same passion in you, and I figured this was a good place to work. A place where I could spend my days hunting down and destroying the people I hate and defending the people who can't defend themselves."

Maggie was lost in his words for a moment. He'd never said any of this before. He'd always come off as a cynical, self-serving, yet highly effective prosecutor.

Coulier sighed. "Well, that's it. That's why I took the job. And what bothers me most right now isn't that you're doing what you believe in. What bothers me is just, well, that they've won. The bullies won this round."

Coulier stared at his open hands in his lap.

"I'm damn proud of you, Madam Governor. I'll do my best to ensure that Warner continues the fight."

He clasped her hand for a moment, then ducked out of the SUV as quickly as he had come.

Maggie sat alone on the leather seat, watching him disappear into the crowd, his last words ringing in her ears.

The bullies won this round. The bullies won this round.

She felt fire seep into her veins, starting in her chest and flowing into her stomach, her hands, and then her cheeks. It was pure, indignant outrage.

To hell with this, she thought. To hell with all of it. She wasn't done. She wasn't quitting now, or ever.

The bullies were going down if it was the last thing she did.

24

Port of New Orleans
New Orleans, Louisiana

Reed heard shouts from the media long before he saw a tight column of security personnel appear, marching with Trousdale toward the podium. With her head held high, Trousdale wore her hair in a simple ponytail, and her minimalist suit joined by black combat boots was something he remembered as a signature of hers from her file.

So this was Muddy Maggie. Reed had to admit, she was pleasant to look at, but it was more than that. Her posture held an air of confidence and command, the sort of inspiring leader that drew out the voters. Today, her face was set in hard, serious lines, but he could imagine how she might radiate if she smiled—if she were on a podium waving and delivering a charismatic campaign speech.

Reed adjusted the wide-brimmed trooper hat and stepped into the crowd, working his way toward the right-hand perimeter as Trousdale marched toward the podium. A couple hundred people had assembled at the dockside to hear Trousdale's address, and a line of state troopers guarded the edges of the crowd, holding shotguns and pepper spray.

A bit aggressive with the shotguns. Maybe this thing is more volatile than I thought.

Near the edge of the crowd, a group of hippies leaned under an oak tree, their checked-out stares and slack jaws betraying their agenda long before their *"Legalize!"* and *"Weed is natural, dude!"* signs. Reed couldn't resist a smirk. Either no one had told them that the dockside workers waving signs fifty feet away were protesting the port closure, or perhaps they just didn't care.

He circled behind the tree and approached the nearest stringy-haired protestor from behind. The guy was wearing a conveniently half-zipped backpack. Reed dipped his hand into his pocket and retrieved the ankle monitor, which was now neatly packaged in a sandwich bag, the red light still blinking every five seconds. Without disturbing the stoned protestor, he dropped the monitor into his open backpack, then stepped away.

After the press conference, Gambit would track the monitor back to whatever pot den Stony retreated to, but by then, Reed would be back in control—the hunter instead of the hunted.

Fifty yards of long strides brought him back through the protestors to the front line of troopers, just fifteen feet from the bulletproof shield. He could see the twin water bottles loaded with shaped C4 just behind the shield, undetected.

Reed wiped a trail of sweat from his forehead. Even in late November, New Orleans was little better than a sauna, and the crowd closing in around him didn't help. He twisted between bodies and worked his way toward the edge of the shield, where more troopers hurried back and forth, snapping at each other and ordering the protestors to step away from the deadline.

He saw Trousdale reappear from the crowd, her skin a paler shade of white than it had been only five minutes prior. Something dark and sticky that had been hurled from the crowd was running down her cheek, and she was escorted at either elbow by troopers burly enough to give Floyd Mayweather a run for his money. They glowered at the protestors and kept their free hands resting on identical Glock 20 pistols.

Geez, these people are tense.

Reed had heard that Louisianans could be wild, but as the chanting grew louder and more pieces of garbage sailed toward the governor, he couldn't help but marvel at the tidal wave of outrage. He wondered if the mob would feel any different after the bombs went off—if they would regret their hostility and mourn their governor.

Trousdale wiped her face with a rag and waved the troopers off as she approached the two steps to the podium. Both officers objected, but she glared them down. Finally, they stepped back, returning her icy glare. It was possible they didn't like her either, Reed thought. Maybe they voted for the other guy. Reed was pretty much apolitical, but he remembered how passionate his mother became over elections. Perhaps these troopers felt more sympathy for the jobless dock workers than they did for their governor.

That could be useful.

Trousdale wiped her face again, then straightened her suit jacket and stepped onto the podium. The crowd erupted in a roar that sounded like something between an angry screech and a chorus of jeers. Trousdale stepped into the middle of the platform, just behind the lectern, and scanned the angry faces.

Reed slipped to the right again, only twenty feet from Trousdale's left shoulder but still on the other side of the shield.

Trousdale held up a hand and leaned toward the microphone. "New Orleans, *I hear you!*"

"Too little, too late, *bitch*!" somebody screamed.

"This is what happens when you elect a woman!"

"Dumb whore!"

Reed flinched, once more astounded by the sheer vitriol of the mob. The reek of liquor drifted from their packed ranks, and he wondered how many of them were wasted beyond their minds.

Do these people even work at the port?

Trousdale extended a finger toward the bearded man who called her a whore. He was spindly and held a paper bag in one hand, only partially concealing the bottle inside.

"Bobby Moore, is that you?" Trousdale demanded. "Shame on you, you son of a bitch. Your mama would roll over in her grave if she saw you now."

Reed blinked. *Did she really just say that?*

The man named Bobby hesitated, uncertainty crossing his face. Somebody in the crowd jammed an elbow into his ribs, and then there was laughter.

"Aww, sheeeeeaat," somebody cursed. "She called you Bobby! Muddy Maggie gonna put a boot in yer ass!"

More laughter, and Trousdale leaned closer to the mic. "Y'all shut up, now! I know you're angry. Dammit, I'm angry, too. You think I wanted this port closed? Y'all shut up, and I'll explain. Shut up, now!"

There was zero fear or intimidation in her voice. She glowered at them, but not with hostility—only command. Reed had never heard a politician talk this way. He wasn't sure if she was beyond caring or if this were just the way of the bayou. Trousdale wasn't a politician, after all. She was a gator farmer's daughter, one of the people, so maybe she knew what they needed better than any political adviser.

The crowd still grumbled, but the shouts began to fade, and the signs were slowly lowered. Reed slid his hand into his pocket and felt for the detonator. He set his jaw and braced himself for the blast—the heat on his face and the dust in his eyes. He didn't want to do this. He liked this swamp girl. She was bold, defiant, totally unyielding, probably a good governor, a great leader, and a vicious enemy . . . of Gambit.

The enemy of my enemy. She is the enemy of my enemy.

Reed closed his eyes and saw his father again in the woods of North Alabama, barely conscious but present enough to look up and recognize his son. There was a lifetime worth of pain and agony and bad things that clouded his father's eyes, but for just a split second, that cloud had parted. Reed saw beyond the trauma of David's shattered psyche and saw his father —a good, strong soul. Just like Trousdale.

A soul who was also the enemy of Reed's enemy.

Reed thumbed the safety switch and placed his hand on the first of the two detonator buttons.

"I'm not here to waste your time with political bullshit," Maggie snapped into the microphone. "You know I'm not like that. I'm here because I know the value of a good job. I'm here because last week I was forced to make a terrible choice to close this port, and you deserve to know why."

Trousdale leaned even closer to the mic, holding the eyes of every person in the now silent crowd, controlling them and consuming their focus.

Reed pressed the button.

The two bottles at the base of the shield erupted in flames, a deafening *boom* ripping skyward as shards of melting plastic and a massive grey cloud filled the air. The bulletproof shield shook, but held, absorbing the brunt of the blast and protecting the crowd, while Trousdale was knocked backward, toppling off her feet and vanishing into the smoke.

A scream burst from the crowd, followed by a chorus of shouts from the troopers, but Reed was already moving. Both hands cleared his pockets, his left hand still clutching the detonator as he circled the shield and leapt toward the podium. A trooper brushed past his elbow just a breath ahead of him. Reed grabbed the man by his collar and hurled him backward with the force of a linebacker, then his feet hit the podium, and he crashed toward the governor.

The air was flooded with smoke, leaving almost nothing visible. Reed lunged forward and almost tripped over Trousdale before he saw her. She sat slumped to one side, coughing and struggling to pick herself up. Reed scooped her up with one powerful heave of his right arm and lifted her slender body over his right shoulder.

After two strides, he lurched forward off the far edge of the podium, landed on his feet, and pressed the second detonator button.

The next blast shook the ground and obliterated the podium, knocking Reed to his knees amid a new deafening roar. Splinters of wood and metal pelted the bulletproof shield and hurtled into the air only inches over his head. He pulled Trousdale closer and dropped the detonator, pushing himself back to his feet and rushing forward. Smoke clouded his way as he slammed between running, screaming protestors, while somebody shouted about blood and sirens screamed in the distance. He could barely see, and his throat was on fire as he crashed between two troopers, took a hard left on the sidewalk, and dashed for the BMW.

25

Gambit leaned closer to the monitor and held his breath as Governor Maggie Trousdale vanished into the first blast. As smoke filled the space behind the bulletproof shield and the governor disappeared from view, a flood of confusion and panic surged through his body. What the hell just happened? Was this part of Montgomery's plan? Why hadn't Montgomery taken the shot yet?

Gambit's hands shook with tension as he turned to another screen and tapped on a keyboard. Montgomery's tracker still signaled from the edge of the crowd, providing an updated location every five seconds. For two blips, it didn't move, and then Montgomery began to track eastward, *away* from the governor.

What the hell? Was he going to shoot at all? Was Trousdale dead?

Another thunderous blast ripped his attention back to the TV. The news media's camera shook, and the reporter screamed as fire and fury blasted into the air behind the shield. This explosion was far more vicious than the first, obliterating the podium and flooding the air with more smoke than a burning stack of tires. Gambit couldn't see anything—not the governor, not her security detail, not Montgomery. The camera fell to the ground, and nothing but dashing feet filled the screen.

"Shit!" he shouted, slamming his hand onto the table. Gambit checked the monitor again and saw that Montgomery was now almost a full block from the port, still moving east. He was gone, slipping away without being caught or verifying that Trousdale was even dead.

Gambit redialed a recent number on his phone, and it rang five times before going to voicemail. He dialed again and once more waited five rings. Montgomery didn't answer.

He forced himself to set the phone down gently. Calm down, he thought. She's probably dead. Who could have survived that blast?

The phone rang, and Gambit's heart lurched, but it wasn't Montgomery. It was Aiden.

The sick feeling in his stomach deepened, leaving him unsteady on his feet. He crashed into his chair and swallowed as the phone rang a second time. Pure animal fear surged into his body, and he hit the answer button.

"Gambit."

"What's happening?" Aiden's voice was unnaturally calm, with no hint of panic slipped into it, and that was somehow even more unnerving than a shout would've been.

"A bomb went off," Gambit said. "Two bombs."

"I know that. The whole world knows that. I'm asking you if she's dead."

There was still no emotion in Aiden's tone, but Gambit felt the bite nonetheless.

"I don't know," he said. "I'm working on it."

"Where is Montgomery?"

"He's tracking east. Seems to be fleeing. I can't get him on the phone."

"Give him half an hour. Keep tracking him, then call again. Once you've confirmed her death, call in the tip to the FBI."

Gambit drew a slow breath and nodded twice. "Of course. I will."

"Gambit?" Aiden's voice assumed a subtle, almost imperceptible edge. It was the edge Gambit had already felt, but now he could hear it.

"Yes?"

"Don't fail me again."

26

The BMW's turbocharged engine roared, launching the car out of the parking lot and onto the street. Reed coughed, his throat still ragged on the C4 smoke as he ran a hand through sweaty hair. He lost the trooper hat during the second blast.

Trousdale sat buckled in the seat next to him, her hands wrapped in duct tape. Another strip of tape covered her mouth, just below panic-filled eyes.

Reed shifted into third and powered through a yellow light, taking another two tight turns and working his way out of downtown. Sirens rang through the air on all sides, but nobody blocked his way. The tinted windows protected them from casual surveillance, but they wouldn't be safe until they were far outside the city.

The BMW hopped onto the highway, and Reed depressed the accelerator, pushing past seventy miles per hour and settling into the left lane. He flipped the cruise control on and leaned back, wiping sweat from his face before taking a gulp of water from a bottle in the cup holder. He turned to Trousdale and held up a finger.

"Don't scream. Do you understand me? If you scream, I'll knock you out."

Trousdale held his gaze for a moment, then nodded. Reed ripped the tape off her mouth, and she winced but didn't scream. He handed her the bottle, and she cradled it between her tied hands and drained it, spilling a few swallows over her smoke-blasted blouse.

The bottle fell onto the floorboard, and she gasped for air. "Who . . . who the hell are you?"

Reed ignored her, swerving around a semitruck and taking I-10 west toward the swamps outside of Lake Pontchartrain.

"What are you doing?" Trousdale snapped.

"Saving your life, believe it or not."

He braced himself for a sarcastic comeback—something he'd become used to from Banks—but Trousdale only frowned, then wiped the back of her bound hand over her chin.

"Why aren't you taking me to the Capitol? Why did you tie me up?"

Fair questions, but he wasn't prepared to answer them. "I'll explain soon. Right now, I need you to remain calm. I won't hurt you."

"Are you a trooper? I don't think you're a trooper."

"No questions."

Reed took an exit that led toward the lake, quickly diving into quiet roads overhung by the drooping limbs of giant trees. Swampy undergrowth surrounded them as they drove farther away from the highway. Reed checked the phone Gambit had given him to ensure he still had a signal. Gambit had already called twice. Reed would answer the third call.

Maggie's heart pounded, but she refused to let the fear show. She sat in the passenger seat next to her captor and kept her arms relaxed, her hands in her lap. The man was well over six feet with broad shoulders and a soldier's expression of cool focus. Ex-military, for sure. Something hard and exclusive. Army Ranger? Maybe. But Rangers operated in groups, as did Navy SEALs and Delta Force. This man was a freelancer—somebody comfortable working alone.

One thing was certain—he was highly trained, and whatever the hell he was up to, it was premeditated. Everything from the bomb blasts to the expedited rescue to the flawless extraction from the city was smooth and sequential. This guy was smart, but he'd made a crucial mistake—he failed to blindfold her. Maggie knew south Louisiana like the back of her hand, every swamp and dirt road, every riverlet and lonely trailer sitting on stilts above muddy ground. This was her home, she knew exactly where she was, and she knew exactly where to hide.

If this guy turned his back for even a moment, she'd be gone like the mucky wind of the swamps, vanished into the trees.

The BMW ground to a halt on the side of a backcountry road, sliding to the side as the tires lost traction on the mud. All around them, tall trees drooped spidery limbs over shallow pond water, with the dying shades of summer green undergrowth slowly collapsing into the mud. Fallen logs rotted against each other, and the occasional fish flipped out of the deeper sections of water to catch a passing bug. Fifty yards away, a small alligator worked his way between the swamp debris before slipping into the water and disappearing from sight.

This was Livingston Parish, situated northwest of New Orleans, and it was the dumbest possible place this man could've taken her. This was her home and oldest stomping ground. Her family's old lake house was only twenty miles away. Friends with shotguns and hair-trigger tempers were all around her. This man would be lucky to survive the night.

The ratcheting sound of the BMW's handbrake ripped through the cabin, and the man turned to her. His eyes were dark, but not as cold as she expected.

"You want another water?"

Maggie shook her head. "No, thanks. Be nice to pee, though."

A flash of amusement crossed his face. "Nah, Governor. You can hold it."

"Governor?" She forced a short laugh. "Dude, I'm the press secretary. You screwed up."

His smirk never faltered. "Nice try, but your picture is all over the news. I know exactly who you are."

Well, it was worth a shot. Maggie leaned back in the seat and lifted her hands in an exhausted, disgusted flip.

"Okay, then. What do you want? Money? Shoulda nabbed a movie star, dude. We're all poor as dirt down here."

He didn't respond, but he held her gaze.

She could see something swirling behind his dark eyes now. Confliction? Hesitation? Or was it simply calculation?

A buzzing sound erupted, and for a moment, the man didn't move. He let the phone buzz twice more, then lifted it from his pocket and nodded at her.

"Stay here." He stepped out of the car, lifted the phone to his ear, and turned his back.

Maggie felt hope leap into her throat. She watched as he took three steps away from the car, his back still turned, the phone held to his ear, then she reached for the door handle and gently pulled it with her bound hands. The heavy German door swung back on silent hinges.

She could hear the man speaking.

". . . I think you have a very good idea where I am. Still tracking me, right?"

One foot out, and then the next. The soles of her combat boots squished in the mud, and she glanced over her shoulder as she began to slip toward the nose of the car.

"She's dead."

That gave her pause, and she glanced back again. Dead? Why would he say that?

"Yeah, I'm sure. Did you see the blast or what? . . . Yeah, I know there was smoke . . . Shoot her? I never said I was gonna shoot her. Why does it matter? She's dead."

Maggie turned away and leaned forward, lowering her shoulders and slowly stepping through the mud, trying to keep the squishing sound to a minimum. She worked her way down the edge of the road, keeping close to the trees and ready to dash into the swamp at a moment's notice.

"Look, you shithead, I did my part. I want my father back. Don't make yourself my next target, Gambit."

Maggie froze, then turned back. The name rang through her mind, ripping like a bullet. *Gambit*. The man she met in a Baton Rouge restaurant only a week prior. A well-dressed man with a suave smile who had threatened her entire family. A man who represented the shadowy, hidden organization Maggie had taken office to destroy. A man who personified corruption in Louisiana.

The animal instincts deep in her psyche screamed for her to run and make for the swamps. To find help and get away.

But her captor was standing *right there*, and he knew where Gambit was. *This man tried to kill you,* a voice in her head said.

But he hadn't. All he'd done was kidnap her and then lie about it to Gambit. What did that mean? Who *was* this man?

He snapped the phone shut, then she saw his shoulders roll back in a frustrated, self-contained gesture. He turned straight toward her, and even as the voices of self-preservation screamed for her to run, Maggie didn't move.

"We need to talk, Governor," he said, his voice betraying no surprise to see her outside the car.

She relaxed her tensed body and nodded slowly. "Yes, I believe we do."

27

They made it to the outskirts of Baton Rouge before Lucy spoke up from the back seat, directing Wolfgang to turn back onto the highway.

"Why?" he demanded. "The arms dealer said Baton Rouge."

"A bomb just went off in downtown New Orleans," Lucy said. "They think the governor was killed."

The cabin of the Mercedes fell deathly quiet for a moment, and Wolfgang looked into the rearview mirror.

"Are you sure it's him?" Banks asked with a slight quiver in her voice.

The other three exchanged looks, then Lucy shrugged. "Maybe not. We have no way of knowing."

"But he did just buy ten pounds of high explosives," Kelly growled.

The cabin fell silent again, and the Mercedes turned southeastward. An hour later, they saw the smoke rising over the Big Easy as the scream of fire engines and police cars filled the air. Wolfgang piloted the coupe as close to the scene of the explosion as possible, but they were quickly stopped by barricades of cops and emergency vehicles. Wolfgang slid the car into a parallel spot, and they piled out, moving down the sidewalk and ducking through the crowds of panicked pedestrians, shouting first responders, and elated reporters. Another two blocks down the street, they slipped through a barricade before topping a slight rise and obtaining a clear view of the Port of New Orleans.

The smoke rose from a spot on the dock only yards from the water. The shattered remains of what may have been a podium lay all over the concrete, while firemen surrounded the mess and showered water on the debris. A bulletproof shield that had surrounded the podium was blasted black with smoke, and flames still licked at the edges of a burned-out dock-side shed ten yards away.

Banks stood at the front of the group, staring out at the chaos as a cold hand of fear wrapped around her stomach. Did Reed blow this place up like a terrorist would do?

"Chaos and destruction," Kelly said, her voice a low snarl behind the burka. "May as well be his signature."

Lucy shoved her on the arm.

"Shut up, Kelly, before I shut you up."

Banks took a half step forward, then stopped as a single tear slipped down her cheek.

They rented adjoining rooms in a slummy hotel north of the city. The clerk behind the counter barely gave the four of them a second glance as Wolfgang paid in cash. The man's attention was distracted by the broadcast on the nearby television, detailing the explosion at the governor's press conference.

Wolfgang and Kelly took one room, and Banks tossed her single back-pack on one of the queen beds in the other, slumping down and staring at her tennis shoes, now torn and dirty. They were nothing like her rows of cute converse back in Atlanta.

"I'm gonna get some food, I guess," Wolfgang said, standing in the doorway between the two rooms. "Any requests?"

Lucy appeared from the bathroom, her makeup removed and her face still glistening with water from the sink. "How about Japanese?"

Wolfgang stared at her a long moment, his eyes growing suddenly soft and distant.

Lucy flicked her hair irritably.

"Don't gawk, asshole. We all look like aliens without makeup."

"No, it's not that. It's . . . nothing. Japanese. Got it." Wolfgang turned away quickly and disappeared through the door.

Lucy rolled her eyes and stepped across the room to sit next to Banks.

"That was weird."

Banks shrugged. "He's a weird guy."

"Yeah, I guess. How are you, honey?"

"I'm good." Banks fiddled with the edge of her sleeve. "Just hungry, I guess."

Her voice betrayed the lie in her words.

"You care about Reed a lot, don't you?" Lucy asked.

"No. I mean . . . maybe, at one point. I just want to know what happened to my father."

Lucy nodded. "I understand that. I lost my father, too, years ago."

Banks looked up. "How?"

"A wreck. He was a race car driver."

"No kidding? NASCAR?"

Lucy laughed. "No. IndyCar. Much faster than NASCAR and much less protection."

"I'm sorry."

Lucy shrugged.

"It happens. Plenty of drivers have died. Except . . ."

Lucy stared down at her hands, then sighed. "Except it wasn't an accident. His fuel lines were sabotaged. A fire broke out in the engine bay. He never had a chance."

"Oh my god. Did they find out who did it?"

Lucy's heartless smile sent a strange chill into Banks's heart.

"Nope," Lucy said. "But I did. And I dealt with it."

Banks hesitated. She had a pretty good idea what "*dealt with it*" meant, but she had to ask. "You mean . . ."

"I took them to the woods, tied them to trees, doused them in racing fuel . . . and set them on fire."

The smile never wavered from Lucy's face, but Banks saw pain and anger behind it.

She looked away. The absolute dichotomy of this woman stunned her to the core. Lucy was so sweet and gentle, yet there was an absolute monster just beneath the surface.

"So you're a killer, too," Banks muttered. "Like Reed."

Lucy nodded. "I worked with Reed, but unlike him, I wasn't forced to take the job."

Banks remembered what Reed had told her about his "arrangement" with Oliver Enfield—thirty kills in exchange for his freedom from death row.

"See, for me," Lucy said, "I have a magnum opus. It's a Latin phrase meaning—"

"It means *great work*. I read *Charlotte's Web*, too."

Lucy laughed. "Yes, that's a great book. Anyway, I believe I have a calling, and that is to rid the world of people like those who killed my father. The bullies, gangsters, and twisted men and women who extort and harm and ruin people's lives. It's why I get out of bed in the morning. I chose to work for Oliver Enfield because, well, killing bad guys is expensive. I needed a way to pay the bills."

Banks sniffed. "How very noble."

Lucy shrugged. "I'm not justifying myself. I choose to do what I do, and I'm not ashamed of it. Last year, I was in Thailand. This guy was running a fake adoption agency. He would 'find families' for orphaned children, or so he claimed. In truth, he was selling them on the black market into the sex trade. Human trafficking at its very worst."

Banks winced. The image twisted her stomach, but she had to ask. "And?"

"And I dealt with it." Lucy winked, but there was still no joy in her eyes.

"The police should do that," Banks said. "Catch the bad guys and bring them to justice."

"Sure. I'm a big supporter of the police. But sometimes things are so messed up, well, there's only one way to fix them. And that's what I do. I fix them. Permanently."

Banks stared at her hands. How much had changed in the past few weeks? Last month, she would've called a woman like Lucy an unthinkable criminal. A serial killer. And technically, she was both of those things. Yet Banks couldn't help imagining a world where good people like Lucy were there for innocent people like those orphans in Thailand. It wasn't easy to stomach, but perhaps it was the best option for a broken world.

Lucy touched her hand, and Banks looked up.

"I know you love him," Lucy said. "I saw it from the moment I first met you. That's not something you should be ashamed of."

"He's a killer, Lucy. He's a bad man. He just assassinated a governor."

Lucy nodded, then leaned forward and kissed Banks gently on the forehead. It was almost motherly.

"Not everything is as it seems."

28

Trousdale remained a cautious twenty feet away from Reed, eyeing him with a semi-suspicious, semi-appraising look. He imagined this woman giving that look to a state legislature or reporters. The sort of look that said she wasn't in the mood for bullshit but was still willing to listen.

She walked across the crunching gravel and extended her bound hands.

"Maggie Trousdale, Louisiana state governor."

Reed took her hand. The grip was a lot stronger than her stature indicated, and she held his gaze with unblinking resolve.

"Reed Montgomery . . ." He trailed off, trying to decide what to call himself. Assassin? Estranged killer? Former Marine? Did it even matter?

He decided it didn't and just let the sentence hang. The pucker of her lips told him she was curious, but she withdrew her hands and rested them over her waist.

"Okay, then, Reed Montgomery. How do you know Gambit?"

He didn't expect that question, but he should have. If Gambit had contracted him to kill Trousdale, it was reasonable that Trousdale would have some idea who Gambit was. Clearly, they had encountered each other before and maybe even had dealings in the past. That was why Gambit wanted her dead, right? She had become a problem for him.

"He hired me to kill you," Reed said.

"But you have a problem killing people."

Reed shook his head. "Not at all. I have a problem killing *good* people."

She nodded, still holding his gaze. Her stare was starting to get to him, so he turned to the back of the car and opened the trunk, producing another two bottles of water and a couple snack bars. He cut the tape from her hands, shut the trunk, and deposited the meal onto the deck lid. Trousdale took the bottle and drained half of it without comment.

"Typically, when I tell somebody that I've been hired to kill them, they have some questions," Reed said.

"What kind of questions?"

"Stupid questions, like, are *you a monster? Or . . . why?*"

"I'm not stupid."

"No, you aren't. And you already know why, don't you?"

She eyed him—that old look of semi-suspicion, semi-appraisal returning.

Reed sighed and folded his arms. "Fine. I'll go first, then. I'm a former Marine who was court-martialed and sentenced to death for executing five civilian contractors in Iraq. They killed one of my friends. While I was on death row, I was given the opportunity to be freed by a criminal organization in exchange for becoming an assassin in their employ and killing thirty people of their choosing. I killed twenty-nine of those people, and on the thirtieth job, everything hit the fan. They wanted me to kill a Georgia state senator by the name of Mitchell Holiday. I didn't want to, for personal reasons. So I blew the whole thing up, and I've been on the run ever since. As it turns out, there were a lot of bad guys between my boss and Gambit, but Gambit was the one who ordered the Mitchell Holiday hit. I have reason to believe that Gambit works for a criminal organization founded by five men, including Holiday, two other guys who died under suspicious circumstances, and my father. Gambit is now holding my father hostage until I kill you, because apparently, you're getting in the way of his organization."

Reed drained the bottle and swept his hand in an open-edged gesture. "That's the CliffsNotes. Your turn."

Trousdale squinted, still suspicious, but her posture was oddly calm.

He'd never encountered a person this calm when they knew they were standing next to a killer. He figured Trousdale's nerves were made of steel.

"If Gambit has your father, and he ordered you to kill me, why didn't you?"

Reed opened his snack bar. "Two reasons. First, like I said, I don't kill good people. Not anymore. Second, if I had killed you, I wouldn't see my father again. Gambit would call the FBI or the police or whoever, and set me up to take the fall for your death, and then he would probably kill my father anyway. I know, because my old employers used the same trick when I failed to kill Holiday. They kidnapped his goddaughter and threatened her life if I didn't finish the job."

"What did you do?"

"I called their bluff and killed a bunch of bad guys. Made a big mess in Atlanta."

She smirked. "So *that's* what all the Atlanta headlines were about."

"Pretty much."

"So now you're calling their bluff again?"

He shook his head and spoke through a mouthful of the snack bar. "Just because they're stupid enough to try the same trick twice doesn't mean they're stupid enough to be outsmarted the same way twice. My only hope of getting my father back is to talk to you, figure out who this Gambit guy is, and how to find him. And I need to do that before he discovers that you're not dead and that a pothead from New Orleans is carrying my ankle monitor in his backpack."

"I'm afraid I'm about to disappoint you. I have no idea who he is."

He crumpled the snack bar wrapper between two powerful palms. "Well, then. You better start talking about what you *do* know. I'm playing nice, but you should know that my father's life means a lot more to me than yours."

She shrugged, still betraying no signs of fear. He could tell she was weighing things out and trying to decide what to say, which meant that she *did* know something. He wondered if he should apply some pressure. Maybe pull out his gun.

No, this woman was smarter than that. He would first have some faith in her and give her a chance to be helpful.

Trousdale looked up. "I'm sure you know that I'm a first-term governor with no prior political experience."

"You're a first-term governor with no prior experience of any sort. I read your file."

"Fair enough. So, I was elected to the office on a campaign of eradicating corruption in the state, on both a governmental and corporate level. We've got a lot of problems in Louisiana. People are struggling to get by. Big corporations are shutting down the small guy left and right, which is capitalism, but they're doing it by cheating the system and exploiting loopholes. Of course, there are lots of problems in Baton Rouge, too. Politicians being bribed and blackmailed. All kinds of shady deals being made in broad daylight. It was my promise to uproot that system and instill some integrity into the state."

She paused as if she expected a question, but Reed didn't answer. He didn't care about her political ideals. He just wanted to know about Gambit.

"So I was elected, and I got down to business, but it wasn't long before I hit trouble. My attorney general was on board with my priorities and was setting up a massive task force to prosecute organized and white-collar crime. He turned up dead not long afterward, his blood laced with poison. A few days later, somebody reached out to me via my website and asked to meet with me. There was something in the note about my former attorney general, so I decided to hear them out. It was Gambit."

"You met him? In broad daylight?"

"Absolutely. He wanted my cooperation in his enterprise—whatever enterprise he's involved in. It was a vague conversation, but I wasn't interested. I shut him down hard, and he threatened my family, so I made it my mission to destroy him."

Reed knew what that anger felt like, when somebody threatens the ones you love most. Apparently, Gambit liked to play that card.

"I hired a new attorney general," Trousdale continued, "and we put together a plan to flush Gambit out. We figured he was operating out of the

Port of New Orleans based on some things he said, so we shut down the port."

"Did it work?"

"No. We had some leads, but as you saw at the protest, people turned against us quickly. We couldn't be transparent about why we shut down the port. The whole thing was a disaster."

"When was this?"

"Two weeks ago."

"I was hired to kill you last week. You must be applying more pressure than you realize."

"I've made some big mistakes," she said. "Shutting down the port, trusting this new attorney general . . . It's cost the state more than I bargained for. My lieutenant governor is currently under investigation for the port closure and the murder of my last attorney general."

"Did he do it?"

She shook her head. "No way. Dan Sharp is a good man. One of the best. He was fully committed to the cause."

Reed grunted. "Then it was probably Gambit, and he probably set up Sharp for the murder, too. Who's next in line for the executive office?"

She frowned. "Why?"

"Gambit wouldn't bring you down unless he controlled your successor. Lieutenant governor is like vice president, right? He becomes governor if something happens to you?"

Trousdale nodded.

"So, Sharp should be taking office right now, but if he is as idealistic and committed as you say, Gambit must know he can't deal with him, either, which is probably why he framed him for the attorney general's death."

A glint of understanding flashed across her face. "I never thought about that. . . ."

"So, who's next in line after Sharp? The new attorney general?"

"No, in Louisiana, the AG is fourth in line. Number three is the secretary of state."

"And?"

Maggie shrugged. "And, I mean . . . he's a good enough guy, I guess. The secretary of state in Louisiana is an elected position. I didn't have much say in who ran. I honestly haven't dealt with him that much, but he always seemed on board with our objectives. Who knows. . . ."

"My guess is Gambit thinks he can deal with him. He gets you out of the way, gets Sharp out of the way, gets your old attorney general out of the way, and now he has a governor who'll play ball and a new AG who won't investigate any of it."

Maggie shook her head. "That's the snag, though. My new AG, Robert Coulier, is a fighter. I call him my pit bull. I brought him on precisely because he prosecutes with so much vigor. The AG slot is also elected in Louisiana, but because Matthews was killed in the middle of his term, I exercised my authority as governor to install a temporary replacement until the end of Matthews's term. Coulier has some majorly rough edges, but he's anti-corruption. Just before the bomb, he actually talked me out of resigning."

Reed puckered his lips and thought for a moment. "Well, maybe Gambit is planning to get rid of Coulier, also. There's any number of possible plays he may have in mind."

Maggie folded her arms and leaned against the car. She dug her toe into the mud, her face twisted into a contemplative frown.

"Why do you care?"

"What?"

"Why do you care what Gambit's up to or what his plans are? If I were in your shoes, I wouldn't give a shit about anything except getting my dad back. Maybe killing Gambit. But none of this other stuff would matter."

Reed opened the trunk again and dug through a bag, producing a pack of cigarettes and tapping one out into his palm.

"Smoke?"

Maggie shook her head. "I don't smoke."

Reed shrugged and slid a cigarette between his teeth. The first drag was ecstasy. It took the edge off of his frayed nerves and helped to slow his still-thumping heart.

He said, "I made a promise to a friend of mine. She's the daughter of one of the five men who started this organization. Her father was killed in New Orleans. The police called it an accident—something about a drunk driver—but it seems likely he was murdered by the same people who wanted Holiday dead and my father doped into insanity. I made her a promise that I would find out, and if necessary, balance the scales."

Maggie held his gaze. "This friend of yours . . . she wouldn't happen to be Holiday's goddaughter, would she?"

Reed took a long drag of the cigarette.

"Doesn't matter who she is. The point is, there's actually a sixth man. His name is Aiden Phillips, and I believe he's Gambit's boss and that he's behind all of this. I want to find him, and you can help me do that."

"How?"

"It's only a matter of time before Gambit confirms that you aren't dead. We need to find him first and apply the necessary pressure."

"Pressure sounds lovely. But how do we find him? He could be anywhere in the country."

Reed flicked the cigarette butt into the mud. "Nope. He's close. He's not gonna risk being too far away from the things he needs to control. I'd bet he's here in New Orleans. After all, if everything you say about his operation is true, and everything I think about Frank Morccelli's death is true, then there's something significant about this city in terms of their operation. It's some sort of base or hub. I'll bet he's a lot closer than you think."

"So, how do you plan to find him in a state this big?"

Reed shut the trunk. "Easy. I'll use his address."

"Right. His address. Why didn't I think of that? Let's just google him. I'm sure there's a listing for *Dastardly Villain*."

"Not google, genius. The car."

"The car?" Maggie squinted at the now muddy BMW.

"Yep. The car. Hop in. I'll explain on the way. You've got some espionage in your future."

29

Something about the explosion bothered Wolfgang all day. He watched the replay on every news outlet he could find while sitting on the edge of the hotel bed amid the wreckage of Japanese takeout, while the girls were huddled in the next room watching some comedy show. Banks was a mess but trying hard not to be. Kelly sat in stony silence, and Lucy . . .

Lucy was something else that bothered Wolfgang. He didn't see it when they first met, probably due to the distraction of having a sword pressed against his neck, but now that he watched her from across the room, the memories came flooding back in painful waves. Memories he hadn't unpacked in years. Memories of another time, in another country, with another woman who bore a resemblance to Lucy that was impossible to ignore. Lucy was smaller than the other woman, and she had green eyes, not grey. She smiled a lot more, too, and certainly had more quirks. But the way she laughed, the quick snap of her wit, and the razor edge of her confidence . . .

Wolfgang looked away from Lucy as his mind traveled back, and he felt the damp sand beneath his feet again. He heard the wash of the waves on the seashore and the rustle of the wind in the palm trees. He felt her soft touch on his skin and the warmth of the glow in her eyes. Her fingers finding their way around his waist, pulling him in, kissing him softly . . .

And then gunshots.

Wolfgang winced and blinked away the memory. He refocused on the television.

The TV flashed to a new view of the bombing, providing welcome relief from the images in his mind. This was the video he was waiting for—the long video, with more detail and clarity. It was shot at a clean angle from the northeast, about twenty feet from the bulletproof shield. That shield had probably saved the cameraman's life, Wolfgang thought. How convenient.

Or intentional.

A few seconds passed. Governor Trousdale began her opening statements, then the first blast went off before a loud crack and a blast of flame. White smoke poured into the air from the base of the shield, and the camera's view of the podium was quickly obscured as the smoke spread and screams filled the air.

Then the second blast, much louder and much more pronounced, threw fire and fury toward the sky. The blast demonstrated all the characteristics of C4 but was much smokier than any C4 Wolfgang had ever used. It was so dirty, in fact, that the explosion failed to knock down the bulletproof shield.

But it wasn't the smoke or even the explosions that triggered his unease. Only milliseconds prior to the second explosion, something caught his attention in the bottom right corner of the screen. A grey flash. Something moving through the smoke and headed toward the podium.

Wolfgang flipped through channels again, searching for a replay of the second bomb. It took him only a few seconds to find one, and this time he focused, waiting for that flash from the side of the screen.

There it was. The flash was a man clad in a Louisiana state trooper's uniform, dashing toward the podium. The face was obscured, but the frame of the shoulders was unforgettable. Unmistakable.

It was Reed Montgomery.

Wolfgang flipped off the TV and stood, scooping up his keys from the nightstand. His pair of Glock 20 pistols, already suspended in shoulder holsters, swung beneath his armpits. Lucy had reluctantly returned them to him before leaving Mississippi.

Wolfgang pulled his jacket on, then stuck his head through the door into the adjoining room. "We're almost out of gas. I'm gonna top off the tank. Be back in a jiffy."

30

Interstate 10
West of Baton Rouge
Louisiana

"How's the car going to help?" Maggie asked.

Reed passed a minivan laden with a tourist family from Oklahoma and flipped on the cruise control.

"When Gambit hired me, I made a list of things I wanted for the job. This car was on the list."

Maggie snorted. "So you juiced him for a nice car. Good for you."

"A nice car would've had a V8 engine and a Chevrolet bow tie. This is a *specific* car."

"What's your point?"

"I told Gambit the car had to have Louisiana plates and local registration."

Maggie puckered her lips, then realization dawned on her face. "Wait . . . local registration. There should be an address on that."

She reached for the glovebox, but Reed shook his head.

"There's an address, but it won't get us anywhere. Gambit isn't that stupid. These plates are probably stolen from a farm truck in a Walmart parking lot. And the registration is just a slip of paper, easily faked. That address could be a random house or an elementary school."

"Okay, so . . ."

"I knew he would fake the registration, so I asked for a foreign car that he wouldn't be able to swipe from a local automotive plant. A car that was specific enough and rare enough that he had to purchase it, in a hurry, from an authorized dealer."

Maggie stared at the dash a moment longer, and then a slow smile spread across her face. "Which would require an address. A real address."

"Yep. Dealerships process new registrations in house, requiring a verifiable address, not to mention a name and a check. All kinds of things. This stuff is all done by computer now, and even if he bought the car in Texas or Florida, I'm willing to bet that the Louisiana DMV already has the paperwork in their system and that Gambit hasn't had a chance to doctor it yet, which gives us a narrow window of opportunity. As governor, I assume you have access to the DMV?"

Maggie nodded. "Sure, I could get in, if you let me go."

"You're not a hostage. You never were. But I think you should give serious consideration to remaining hidden. Once people know you're alive, you'll be put under protective custody, which will limit your ability to do anything about Gambit. And also—"

"And also he'll know I'm alive and kill your father."

Reed nodded. "Which isn't your problem, but . . . I could use your help."

"Don't worry. I'm not as dumb as most politicians. And anyway, I'm already outside the law. I may as well take advantage."

Reed let out a mental sigh. There was always the possibility that Maggie wouldn't play along. He was impressed by her mental fortitude and quiet confidence. If she had wanted to call the police, he couldn't have let that happen—not while his father was a prisoner with a knife at this throat.

"I guess we're headed to Baton Rouge, then?" she said.

"Yes. We—or you—need to get inside the DMV and pull those records without anyone knowing. Is there anybody you can trust? Somebody who would be discreet?"

Maggie's shoulders slumped. "Not anymore. Sharp may have, or my chief of staff, but they're gone now. It's just me."

"Okay, then. I assume you have some kind of ID? Something to get into buildings with?"

"Yeah, I've got some codes and stuff. The DMV should be a relatively unrestricted building, actually. Just a basic security system and electronically locked doors. The only trouble is that my code will be logged, which will expose us, eventually."

"Right. But by then, it won't matter. I'll have my father back, and you'll have risen from the dead."

Maggie nodded, but the gesture lacked enthusiasm. Reed wondered for the first time if she really wanted to be governor. He assumed that anybody who ran for office longed for the power and prestige, but maybe not Maggie. Maybe Maggie was burdened by the office. Maybe she was truly one of those people who just wanted to serve and was now broken by the extreme corruption and cynicism of the world around her.

Maggie folded her arms, then wiggled her hips deeper into the plush leather.

"It really is a nice car. Could use a sunroof."

"I ordered it without one."

"Why?"

Reed grunted. "In case I roll it."

"In case you *roll it*? Should I be driving?"

He offered a weak smile.

"I always preferred trucks," she said. "Or Jeeps. Anything four-wheel-drive that I could get muddy in."

"Muddy Maggie . . ." Reed mused, a clear question hanging at the end of the sentence.

"Where did you hear that?"

"It was in your kill file. I read all about you and your campaign. Pretty inspiring stuff. I would've voted for you."

He waited, hoping she might explain why she ran. He wasn't sure why, but he found the subject intriguing.

"I don't feel like Muddy Maggie anymore," she murmured. "Dirty Maggie, maybe."

Reed noticed her slump in the seat. She looked tired. Sure, the remnants of the blast dust she was unable to wipe away didn't help her general appearance, but deeper than that, there was some level of weariness that saturated her very bones.

To hell with this guy, whoever he was. Whether it was Gambit or Aiden or somebody even worse, this entire organization had sucked the life out of too many good people, starting with his own father, and Banks's father, and then Holiday. Now Dick Carter and Muddy Maggie and all the nameless, faceless innocents in between.

Whoever he was, and wherever he was hiding, Reed was going to find him. He was going to wrap his hands around this man's throat and spit in his face as he choked his life away.

31

Baton Rouge, Louisiana

Another humid night fell over Louisiana's capital city, shrouding the sidewalks in mist and leaving every bright thing a distorted orb of itself. The Department of Motor Vehicles in downtown Baton Rouge wasn't called the DMV, it was called the Louisiana Office of Motor Vehicles, which was pretty much the same thing, but Reed noticed that most things in Louisiana were called something unique. Maggie explained that it had to do with the origins of state law. Most states in the US traced their legal system back to the foundations of English Common Law, whereas Louisiana traced theirs back to French and Spanish civil law, which was itself a derivative of ancient Roman law. Maggie seemed to know a lot about the state, how it operated, and what made it special. As they crossed into downtown and the clock slid past eleven p.m., Reed couldn't help but notice the longing, loving look that she cast toward each passing building, whether it was a library or a sandwich shop.

This is her home. She actually, truly loves this place and these people.

In Reed's brief experience with politicians, most of them were something worse than the scum of the earth. The kinds of men who sat behind mahogany desks with guts that spilled out over their expensive trousers, pontificating about the needs of poor people and the necessities of a strong military without really understanding or caring about either. The kinds of people who deployed men like himself into faraway countries to do horrible things with no concern about the collateral damage.

But Maggie was different. She did care. She understood her people, their unique problems, and what they needed in a leader. This woman was ready for war, completely unconcerned with the fact that she was putting her entire political career, and maybe her life, on the line to hunt down and destroy the enemies of her people.

He admired that and wondered if he could ever be the same. He wondered if he'd ever live long enough to find out.

They parked the BMW a couple blocks from the DMV, or whatever it was called, and walked together along quiet sidewalks.

"If we were in New Orleans right now," Maggie said, "there would be music and dancing and plenty of great food."

Reed grunted. He found little appeal in music or food right now. All he wanted was his father back, to steal away the man who was stolen from him, and then to put his boot on Gambit's neck until he felt the bones snap.

Across the street from the squat, two-story motor vehicle building was a semi-circular flagstone park with a fountain, some trees, and two park benches.

Maggie stopped Reed next to the fountain and scooped a phone from her pocket.

"What's your number? I'll text you if I have problems."

Reed shook his head and withdrew a burner phone from his coat. "Use this. My number is already programmed inside. You got the VIN?"

Maggie took the phone and unfolded her hand to reveal a scrap of paper with the BMW's vehicle identification number scratched on it, then she set off toward the darkened building.

Reed settled onto one of the park benches, adjusted his jacket around the SIG handgun in his belt, and studied the building. If Maggie were detected, there would be very little he could do short of an armed assault. It wasn't like she would be in any danger, but she would almost certainly be recognized, and that would unravel the whole thing.

Moments ticked into minutes, and Reed's phone buzzed. Maggie texted him.

I'M IN.

He closed the phone and leaned forward again, suddenly craving a cigarette. It was a habit he couldn't shake, although he hadn't actually tried very hard. The nicotine might be poison, but all things considered, it felt a lot less lethal than his next gunfight.

Reed shook a smoke out of the pack and felt for his lighter. The flame danced under the tip, and his lungs flooded with the relieving glory of the drug.

"Hello, Reed."

The voice came from behind, barely inches away. Reed bolted out of the bench and jerked the SIG from his belt, already knowing he was too late. The voice was too close, right in his blind spot, already on top of him and ready to kill.

Reed whirled, raising the gun and placing his finger on the trigger as he braced for the searing pain from the bullets that would rip through his body, hot and heavy, shredding flesh and bone.

But they didn't come. As Reed completed his spin, the sights of the pistol came to rest over a tall, trim man standing a yard behind the bench. He was dark-haired and dressed in a peacoat, with his hands casually jammed into the pockets.

Reed recognized those piercing eyes and that casual smirk immediately. It was Wolfgang Peirce, a.k.a. *The Wolf*, the killer who had chased him through the mountains of North Carolina, had almost killed both him and Banks during a reckless car chase along the Tail of the Dragon pass near the Tennessee border, and then showed up out of nowhere in Nashville.

The killer who had gunned down Salvador, Reed's only link to Gambit's organization at the time.

Reed lowered the muzzle of the gun, his finger still resting on the trigger. Wolfgang displayed no signs of aggression, remaining relaxed with his shoulders slumped, his easy smirk hanging like a ghost at the corners of his mouth.

"You're edgy, Reed. You should see a therapist."

Reed licked his lips, suddenly aware that the cigarette was gone but unconcerned with where it had fallen.

"What do you want?"

Wolfgang tilted his head, holding Reed's gaze for a long moment, then he lifted his hands out of his pockets. Reed's trigger finger tensed, but The Wolf's hands were empty.

"Just to talk. Like we did that time in Chattanooga at dinner. Seems like I snuck up on you then, also."

"Yeah, you've got a habit of doing that, don't you?"

Wolfgang shrugged. "It's kind of my job. May I sit?"

Reed hesitated, chewing his lip. Every war-honed instinct in him ordered his finger to press the trigger and blow this guy away. Tonight marked the third occasion that Wolfgang had got the jump on him—fourth if he counted that business in Nashville. Each time, Wolfgang could've easily killed him, but thanks to fate, or one of Wolfgang's bizarre rules, he never had.

"What's to stop you from popping a bullet into my head?" Reed asked.

Wolfgang checked his watch. "It's only five minutes to midnight. You know I don't kill after midnight."

"So you've said. I still don't know why."

"My mother used to tell me that nothing good happens after midnight. Words to live by, my friend."

Reed hesitated, his finger gently massaging the face of the trigger. He lowered the gun and backed up without taking his sight off The Wolf. He sat down on the far edge of the seat and gestured to the adjacent park bench five feet away.

Wolfgang dusted off the bench before sitting down and kept his hands exposed in his lap.

"I guess the governor's inside?"

Reed squinted. "I don't know what you're talking about."

"Sure you do. That was your business in New Orleans. It had your fingerprints all over it. Plus, I saw you on the video when you dashed in to push the governor off the podium, right before the second blast. Mexican C4, right? Smokey stuff. Smokey enough to conceal your movements and make a person think the governor must have gone up with the second blast."

Reed chewed his lip again, then reached into his pocket for a fresh smoke.

Wolfgang continued to smirk.

"Honestly, Reed, it was a nice piece of work. And it'll fool most people until the medical examiners find zero biological trace of the governor's 'vaporized' body. Which won't be long."

"Get to the point," Reed snapped. "Why are you here?"

"Don't you want to know how I found you?"

Reed did, very much, but he wasn't going to give Wolfgang the benefit of that curiosity.

"I don't really care. I just want to know why."

"Always the blunt one, aren't you? Okay, I'm here because last week somebody left a very valuable item on my doorstep, with a note claiming that you have more of this item. I'm here to collect it."

Reed's face twisted into a frown. "What the hell are you talking about?"

"I think you know."

"What item?"

"A chemical solution designed to promote the organic modification of DNA structure."

Wolfgang held his gaze, the smirk having melted away like ice on a hot day.

"Whatever you're talking about, I don't have it," Reed said.

Wolfgang rubbed his chin. "Maybe you do and don't know it yet. What are you doing in Baton Rouge, Reed? Who hired you to kill the governor?"

Reed snorted. "You think I'm going to discuss that with you?"

"I know about your father. I know he went insane in prison and that three days ago he went missing out of his facility in North Alabama. I also know you were there and that you planned to break him out. But something went wrong."

A cold hand of uncertainty closed around Reed's stomach. He resisted the urge to swallow and slowly lifted the cigarette to his lips, lighting it with his left hand while the SIG remained clamped in his right.

He took a long puff. There was only one way Wolfgang could know those things. Only one way he could have any idea about what happened at the prison.

"Banks is with you," Reed said.

Wolfgang nodded. "She is. Along with . . . other people. People who are very concerned about you, Reed. People who want to help you."

"I don't need help. And I don't want Banks dragged into this. I left her in Alabama for a reason."

Wolfgang laughed. "Don't be so sexist, Reed. Believe me, she's the one doing the dragging. Well, her and her *squad*. Did you know that's what women call themselves these days? When a group of them go on a power trip, they call it a *squad*. Scary, right? Like Marines."

Reed took a drag from his cigarette, holding Wolfgang's gaze without comment.

Wolfgang leaned forward, interlacing his fingers. "I don't want her hurt, either. I don't want anybody hurt. That's why I'm here. The substance that arrived on my doorstep is incredibly valuable, but in the wrong hands, it could also be incredibly dangerous. You need to work with me."

Reed finished the smoke and flicked the butt onto the sidewalk. "I can't help you, Wolf. I've got my own problems."

Wolfgang frowned, then a realization dawned across his face. "They have your father, don't they?"

Something must have flashed across Reed's face because Wolfgang's expression morphed into what looked like genuine compassion.

"Let me help you, Reed. We can get him back, together."

Reed shook his head. "Not a chance, hotshot. This isn't your war. If you start bumbling around, they'll kill him."

"Give me some credit. If I can sneak up on you, I must be pretty good."

"It's not about that. It's about family. He's my father, and I'm getting him *back*."

Reed regretted the words as soon as they left his lips.

Wolfgang cocked his head and bit his lip, then he sighed.

"I've read his medical files, Reed. I'm a doctor, believe it or not. Your father . . . he's gone. His brain is barely alive."

Reed sat forward, the gun jerking. "That's not true!"

Wolfgang didn't flinch.

"I saw him," Reed continued. "I saw him in the woods. He recognized me. There was a toy car in his jail cell. It was something he used to own . . . something he *remembered*."

"People like your father may occasionally experience flashes of memory, but trust me, you are being manipulated. Whoever is holding your father is playing games."

Reed locked his jaw and kept the gun pointed at Wolfgang's gut.

"I think it's time you left before I change my mind about killing you."

Wolfgang replaced his hands in his pockets and stood. He stepped to the end of the bench, then turned back.

"She loves you, you know. Banks does. I saw it in her eyes the first time she said your name."

Reed's glare blazed, but he said nothing.

"You're burning down the world in this war of yours. And I get it, Reed. Lines have been crossed. But there's no reason for you to walk this path alone. I want to help you."

"You want what *you* want," Reed snapped.

Wolfgang nodded. "That's true, but we can help each other. We *need* to help each other."

"You want to help me? Get Banks out of here. She's an innocent bystander, and you know it. Get her someplace safe, then maybe we'll talk."

"Fair enough," Wolfgang said. "I'll do what I can."

Reed stared him down and didn't answer. Wolfgang turned into the shadows and vanished like the ghost he was, fading into the midnight mist.

A few moments later, Reed heard the familiar growl of the big Mercedes and then the squeal of tires.

He lowered the gun, an overwhelming wave of conflicted emotions passing over him. Fear and pain and loneliness crushed down on him like the weight of the world. He wanted to sob or scream or shoot something.

But he pressed the urges back, shoving every tired and aching emotion deep into his soul, into the darkness, into the place where everything was numb enough to allow him to keep going.

Footsteps clicked against the sidewalk, light and fast. Reed replaced the SIG into his holster and stood as Maggie burst through the mist, her eyes alight in victory.

"I found it!" she said. "I found an address."

32

The hotel door opened without a sound under Wolfgang's gentle push. The room was dark, lit only by the soft glow of an alarm clock. From the adjoining room, Wolfgang could hear Kelly snoring fitfully, struggling for air through her disfigured face. All else was quiet.

He pressed the door shut and sighed, moving to unbutton his peacoat.

"Hello, Lucy," he muttered.

Lucy was invisible, but he could feel her presence from the darkened corner of the room.

"Where have you been?" she said.

He slid off the coat and deposited it on the TV stand, then sat down on the edge of the bed and began to untie his shoes.

"I told you. I went for gas."

"Three hours ago."

"I took a drive. Cleared my head. I'm allowed to do that, you know."

She didn't respond, but the silence hung with suspicion.

He looked into the corner but still couldn't see her.

"I don't think you're being honest with me," she said. "I hope you remember what happened last time you were dishonest with me."

Wolfgang couldn't help but squeeze his legs together. Hell would freeze over before he let any of these crazy women tie him to a chair again.

"I've got nothing to discuss with you, shadow woman. It's past my bedtime."

A sudden click resulted in a bright flood of light. Banks emerged from the adjoining room, her hair tousled and her eyes blazing.

"Where the hell did you go, dude? We needed you here. We need to strategize about next steps!"

The snoring faded, and a moment passed before Kelly appeared. She was dressed in her typical black garb, minus the headpiece. Her mutilated features sent a wave of nausea through Wolfgang's stomach, and he looked away.

"Now that we're all present," Lucy said from the chair in the corner, "you should come clean."

Wolfgang shot her a deadly glare. She sat in the chair, one leather-clad leg crossed over the other, her hands held loosely in her lap. The picture of condescending confidence.

Wolfgang looked away, then sighed.

"Okay, fine. I went downtown to investigate the blast."

"And?" Banks snapped. "We should've gone together."

Wolfgang laughed. "Sure. A bomb goes off, and then Miss Arabia shows up? I don't think so."

"That's racist," Lucy said.

"It's reality. You think these cops wouldn't flip out if they saw her poking around dressed like that? I had to go alone."

"What did you find?" Banks demanded.

Wolfgang hesitated. Now was the moment of truth. Did he trust Reed, or did he rely on "the squad"? These women might be tough and smart and resilient, but the path between him and finding the source of whatever was left on his doorstep was a path for a lone wolf—not a pack.

"I think it's time we left Louisiana," he said quietly.

"*What?*" Banks snapped.

"Listen," he said, "I get it. You want to find Reed. You want answers. I don't know for sure what's happening down here, but I do know that Reed set off that bomb today, and I do know that the governor is missing and maybe dead. It's about to get really hot around here, and we don't need to get mixed up in that."

"Damn coward," Kelly snarled. "You're trying to save your own skin."

"No, I'm not. I'm thinking more than one step ahead. And I'm telling you, the path we're traveling isn't leading us to Reed."

"You found him," Lucy said in a soft but steely voice.

"What?" Wolfgang scratched his arm and looked away.

"You found Reed. That's where you went tonight."

Wolfgang hesitated, his mind spinning as he frantically searched for a plausible denial, but it was already too late. His hesitation had lasted too long.

"We need to leave." He turned to Banks. "Especially you."

"*Me?*" She snapped. "Why me?"

"Because Reed said so," Lucy said, her voice still calm. "Because Reed cares about you, just like I said he did. And he's trying to distance you. Right, Wolfgang?"

Wolfgang clenched his jaw. He'd lost complete control *again*, and there was little he could do except walk out.

"Look, you do what you want." He slid his feet back into his shoes. "But I'm telling you, you're on a fool's errand. I'm done."

An iron grip descended on Wolfgang's shoulder, and he looked up to see Banks standing next to him.

She pivoted around to stand in front of him and then placed her free hand on her hip. "You're not going anywhere, Wolf. We're going to get in that car, and we're going back to town. We're going to *find* Reed, and we're going to *find* some answers. All of us."

33

J. Edgar Hoover Building
Washington, D.C.

Special Agent Rufus "Turk" Turkman was one energy drink away from collapsing from a heart attack . . . or extreme exhaustion; it was difficult to tell the difference. He crushed another Red Bull can between powerful fingers and flung it into a nearby trash can, then he ran his hand through short, dirty hair. He needed a shower. He needed no less than ten hours of sleep. He needed a hot meal that wasn't manufactured inside the FBI Headquarters' cafeteria.

But more than anything, he needed a lead.

For three weeks, Turk and his boss, Special Agent Matthew Rollick, had chased down clues related to the murder of State Senator Mitchell Holiday. Rollick had been working a possible corruption case involving Holiday prior to the senator's death, but once the case spilled into bloodshed, additional manpower was needed, and Turk was brought in.

Only months out of Quantico, he was a brand-new, unbroken field agent ready to prove his worth. After eight years in the Marine Corps, Turk was used to the jokes about jarheads, and he was eager to prove them wrong. He was ready to demonstrate that he could be lethal with more than just an M27 automatic rifle.

But nothing—not the Marines, not Iraq, not Quantico—could prepare him for what he was about to step into. Turk leaned back in the chair and closed his eyes, his mind drifting back to only five days prior, when he stood in the midst of a steady snowfall outside Cheyenne Regional Airport in Wyoming, drew his FBI-issued Glock handgun and pointed it at his oldest friend.

Reed Montgomery.

Turk still couldn't believe he had been there. Reed was Turk's fireteam lead in Iraq, back when they were both Force Recon Marines running intel ops behind ISIL lines. They fought, killed, and bled together in that godforsaken sandpit for more than three years, deployment after deployment.

Reed was more than a great soldier—he was a war hound, a brutal fighter who drew energy from long missions with little food, water, or sleep. The more gunfire, the better. The steeper the odds, the harder Montgomery fought. He didn't actually care about life, Turk thought. He just cared about winning.

Was it patriotism? A death wish? Turk didn't know. At first, the battle-crazed look in Reed's eyes scared the shit out of him. He almost requested a transfer.

But then there had been that mission deep behind ISIL lines, to the very outskirts of the war-shattered city of Fallujah. Everything went wrong on that op. Their cover was blown, their radios failed, they were cornered in unfamiliar territory with ISIL on four sides and the nearest American troops miles away.

They were going to die. Turk believed it. He even accepted it.

But not Reed. Corporal Montgomery didn't accept failure, and he was completely unimpressed by the surge of jihad fighters that closed on their position. Reed became something that night that Turk still wasn't sure was real—a complete, total fighting machine. As the bodies piled up and Reed switched from his exhausted M4 to a captured AK-47, he never seemed to tire. Hundreds of rounds turned into thousands, the sky filled with the roar of the gunfire, and then ...

And then they retreated. To this day, Turk wasn't sure what caused the

ISIL fighters to fall back. They had to know only three Marines were standing in front of them.

By the time the sun rose over the empty wasteland of western Iraq, Reed Montgomery had led his fireteam out of that hellhole and pushed the three of them through a brutal eight-mile run back to friendly territory.

They made it to camp, completed their debrief, took twelve hours to rest and refit, and then that crazy SOB was ready to go again.

Turk felt something hot sliding down his cheek and brushed it away as he reached for another Red Bull.

"What happened to you, Reed?" he whispered as he stared at the spread of high-resolution photographs on his desk. They were pictures of war and chaos, right here in the heartland of the United States. From Atlanta to North Carolina to Nashville, gunfights, bodies, and burning cars—the signature of a born fighter.

Turk knew nothing had happened to Reed Montgomery. He hadn't changed. Reed had simply come home, and intentionally or otherwise, brought the warrior with him.

He remembered the last time he saw Reed. It was in a military court-room in Washington, D.C., where Reed was convicted of five counts of first-degree murder. It happened in Baghdad after their last mission together. A Humvee driver, some young kid from Georgia, joined the Marines to pay for college. Turk couldn't remember her name, but he remembered the moment Reed looked into her terrified eyes and said, "Just drive. We'll take care of the rest."

That scared private didn't know it at the time, but when Reed said those words, he was accepting her under his umbrella of protection—the same umbrella that covered Reed's fireteam. The umbrella that said "I'll get you out of here."

So when that private was later found in a pool of her own blood, having been mugged, raped, and beaten to death by a group of five civilian contractors, Reed's reaction was predictable. He loaded his rifle and gunned them down like a group of jihadists.

But of course, Uncle Sam wasn't paying Reed to gun down Americans, regardless of what they had done. So Reed was arrested, court-martialed, and sentenced to death. The last time Turk saw his old friend was when they stripped the USMC patches off his arms and dragged him away to die.

Turk sipped the Red Bull and stared at the photographs. After that moment, he assumed he would never see Reed again, which was why he never expected to find Reed at the very heart of this investigation.

Turk wiped his tired eyes and leaned forward, studying the photographs again. There was no logic to the warpath Reed had carved through the south. Of course, there had to be a reason. Reed always had a reason. But there were far, far too many question marks over the last three years.

For instance, how the hell did Reed slip out of both the military and civilian prison systems and simply disappear? There were no documented escape attempts and no missing person reports. He was simply a prisoner . . . and then he wasn't.

"Where did you go, Reed?" Turk whispered.

A shoe clicked against the utilitarian floor outside of Turk's cubicle, and he looked up to see Rollick stepping in. His boss's face was cold and angry, with black bags under his eyes and exhaustion lines creasing his cheeks.

"Pack it up, Turk. We're done."

Turk blinked. "Say what?"

"Pack it up. Everything. We've been pulled from the case."

Rollick started down the hall, and Turk jumped to his feet and bolted after him, a sudden surge of adrenaline bringing life back to his body.

"Wait! Pulled? What do you mean, *pulled*?"

Rollick shoved a cell phone in Turk's face and showed him a video, preloaded and already playing. It was of a female politician standing on a podium. He didn't recognize her, but she was clearly an executive. Everything about her demeanor said so.

Turk flinched as the bomb went off.

Smoke filled the screen, and Rollick lowered the phone.

"Your boy just set off a bomb in New Orleans. That woman is the governor of Louisiana."

Rollick headed toward the elevator.

"Wait . . . I don't understand. Is she dead?"

"There's no body. We think she's missing. But Montgomery's face was captured by a parking lot security camera near the scene of the crime, and we've got a battered Louisiana state trooper who says a man matching Montgomery's description attacked him, knocked him out, and stole his uniform."

Rollick hit the elevator button.

"So . . ." Turk struggled for his next thought. Even with the Red Bull and the adrenaline, his mind moved in slow motion. "We have to go to New Orleans. He could be close."

Rollick shook his head. "Nope. This has spilled far beyond a murder case. Counterterrorism is taking over. We're done."

"Like hell we're done!" Turk's deep Tennessee voice rose to a boom.

The elevator door rolled open, and Rollick stepped inside.

Turk put his boot over the threshold, blocking the door.

"Rollick, I'm not quitting. Reed is out there somewhere, and I don't know what the hell he's up to, but so help me God, I'm bringing him in. Do you hear me?"

Rollick met his eyes. The anger was still there, but he looked exhausted more than anything.

"Turk, take it from an old man. Follow orders. You've been pulled. Be happy you weren't fired."

Turk noticed for the first time that Rollick's FBI pin was missing from his lapel, and there was no bulge beneath his jacket where his handgun should've been.

"Wait, you . . ."

Rollick shrugged. "People are dead. Somebody has to take the fall."

He punched the button for the parking garage and nodded at Turk.

"Good luck, buddy. You've got the makings of a great agent."

Turk stepped back and watched as the door rolled shut. The room around him was silent—whatever agents worked on this floor had already gone home for the night, leaving him standing alone beneath the flickering white light.

A knot twisted in his stomach, and he blinked back the exhaustion. For a moment, he stared at the elevator button, debating whether he should press it and follow Rollick to the garage.

No. Rollick was gone; there was nothing to do about that. But not Turk. He was still there, and he was still an agent.

Turk turned and fast-walked back to his cubicle, his mouth setting in a hard line. He scooped the photographs into a box, tossed his laptop on top, and grabbed his car keys from the desk.

Montgomery had never quit, no matter the odds. Turk would be damned if he folded now.

34

Reed and Maggie spent the night in a run-down motel located just south of the highway. The BMW stuck out like a sore thumb at the disheveled joint, but it was still the best hiding place either of them could think of on short notice, and the front desk didn't ask for identification.

As the sun broke through the grimy window, Maggie awoke, curled up on one of the beds with an aching back and pounding head. Reed sat in one of the dingy armchairs, staring through the window at the parking lot. His eyes were rimmed red, and he held an empty whiskey glass. She wasn't sure if he had slept at all, but when he spoke, his voice was clear.

"Gambit called. I stalled him. They still think you're dead."

Maggie blinked her sleep away. "Isn't it obvious there wasn't a body in the debris?"

"I'm sure, but it's only been a few hours. The cops aren't ready to pronounce you missing yet. They'll wait until noon, I'd guess."

"At which point Gambit will be a problem."

Reed nodded, then set the glass on an end table and stood up. "Let's ride."

They piled back into the BMW after a quick breakfast of oatmeal pies from the hotel vending machine, and Reed turned them east toward New Orleans. Maggie had washed the blast smoke from her face, then found a Saints T-shirt, an LSU ball cap, and a pair of jeans from a local thrift store. She was unsatisfied with the disguise but also wondered how many people actually knew what their governor looked like.

Hopefully not many.

As they drove, Maggie used one of Reed's phones—he seemed to have several—to locate the address she had stolen from the DMV the night before. It was an office building located in downtown New Orleans, not far from the French Quarter in an old business district. It was the kind of place populated by law firms and accountants.

"It's some kind of company called BANO—Business Associates of New Orleans," she said. "I think it's an entity representation service, which makes sense because the BMW was purchased last week by *ABC Consultants, LLC,* and ABC doesn't pop up on any Google searches."

Reed grunted. None of this surprised him. He expected the car to be owned by a company, not an individual.

"So ABC uses BANO as their registered agent," he said, "which allows them to use BANO's address as their own on any legal paperwork, such as a vehicle bill of sale. Another layer of anonymity for anybody wanting to remain private."

"Or hidden," Maggie said. She had already navigated to the Louisiana Secretary of State website and looked up *ABC Consultants, LLC.* ABC popped up immediately as an active registration, but when she opened the file, the only address listed belonged to BANO.

"That adds up," she said. "Gambit's organization runs their elicit operations through the LLC but they use a registered agent to shield their exact identities. Pretty shady."

"Not necessarily," Reed said. "Lots of companies are run that way. The whole point of an LLC is to limit the liability that a business owner is exposed to. But yes, it definitely feels like a shell company for some type of criminal organization. I mean, who the hell names a company *ABC Consultants*? What does that even mean?"

"Even if ABC is a shell company, BANO must hold records of who owns ABC and what their actual address is. They're not gonna give that sort of information away, though. It's confidential."

Reed grunted. "I can be very persuasive."

Maggie rubbed her thumb against the leather-clad armrest of the BMW. In the back of her mind, a voice screamed that this was all very, very wrong. Much worse than following Coulier's semi-criminal methods of closing the port. This *was* criminal. And it was dangerous. This man she sat beside was a killer by profession, and following him along this path would result in further corruption. She could leave now, return to the police, be ushered back into the Capitol, and resume her original plan of making things right.

But where would that lead her? Would she really make any progress toward finding Gambit? In the fifteen-odd hours that she'd been "dead," she had made more headway on tracking down this scum than she had in months of being governor. Sure, her new methods were shady, but they worked. She was now only hours away from wrapping her metaphorical hands around Gambit's throat.

Wouldn't that be better for the state? Wouldn't it be more productive for her to finish her speech by announcing the takedown of one of the state's largest, most sordid criminal enterprises?

Then she could explain everything—the port closure and the chaos inside the Capitol. She could exonerate Dan Sharp and get him back to work as her lieutenant governor. If she could just put her thumb on Gambit, everything could be turned around in the blink of an eye.

She wouldn't quit now. She was too close and too determined.

35

Business Associates of New Orleans was housed on the second floor of a French-style office suite, fully equipped with decorative metal railings and overhung by towering oak trees. Reed and Maggie found a café on the first floor of the facing building, and Reed motioned to one corner of the dining room.

"Wait here," he said. "I'll be back in ten minutes."

Maggie sat down, casting a wary glance around the room for anybody she recognized. It was paranoia, she knew. It was extremely unlikely that anybody would recognize her here, dressed this way, sitting alone in a dusty corner, but still, she couldn't shake the feeling that if she were discovered, things would be much worse.

It was a dumb feeling, she decided. She was in control now more than ever.

"What are you gonna do?" she asked.

Reed started to the door. "Find out who the hell owns ABC Consultants."

Maggie settled into a booth and watched Reed slip through the door and jog across the street. She didn't really mean *"What are you going to do?"*

but "How *are you going to do it*?" Even as she rephrased the question in her mind, she knew he wouldn't have answered.

Who was this man from the shadows, dark and brooding, with the demeanor of a cold-blooded killer? She found it easy to believe that he was both a Marine and a professional assassin at one time or the other. She also found it easy to trust him, and that alarmed her. There was no objective, concrete reason to trust Reed. Was she playing the fool and stepping into his trap?

"Ma'am?" The voice came from her left, slow and syrupy like only New Orleanians spoke. Maggie blinked and looked up, then looked down just as quickly.

The waitress stood next to the table, a pad in her hand, one eyebrow raised.

"Just coffee, please. Black."

"Sure thing, dahlin'."

The waitress disappeared, and Maggie let out a strained breath. She had to chill out, she thought. This tension was pointless and highly destructive. She needed to focus and think about what she would do when they found Gambit.

Maggie turned back to the window and watched as Reed ducked through the main door of the office suite, vanishing from sight. He walked without a trace of hesitation—a man with nothing to fear, or perhaps, a lot to lose.

The coffee cup clicked against the tabletop, and Maggie took a sip without looking up.

A voice came from the TV set mounted near the ceiling. ". . . we interrupt this program to deliver a breaking news bulletin . . ."

Maggie watched as replays from the Saints' last game faded to a newscaster sitting behind a polished desk. She recognized the face immediately as the chief anchor for New Orleans's most prominent local station.

"In a shocking turn of events for the recent bombing in downtown New Orleans, Chief Richards of the NOPD is now reporting that Governor Maggie Trousdale's body was *not* found in the ashes."

The screen switched again, this time to the swarthy face of Chief Richards standing behind a podium in front of the police department. He was a big man with broad shoulders, eyes that were easy to trust, and a sad face. Maggie knew him well and liked him. He was good at his job.

"Our forensics experts have completed their review of the blast site," Richards said, his voice a painfully slow drawl, "and have determined that Govenah Trousdale's body is not among the ashes."

Camera flashes lit the screen, followed by a peppering of questions from reporters.

Richards held up his hand.

"At this time, no. At this time, we have no evidence that indicates that Govenah Trousdale was killed, and we are now classifying her as a missing person."

Maggie's stomach twisted into successively tighter knots. She shifted in her seat and watched as the screen switched back to the anchor. He opined for a moment longer about the situation at the blast site, and Maggie tried to block out his voice.

So this was it, she thought. Gambit would know she was alive, which meant escalated pressure on Reed and an all-out manhunt from the NOPD, the State Police, and the FBI. Everybody would be involved.

They would come for Reed. They would run him into the ground, not stopping, not sleeping until Maggie was found.

Her head told her that it wasn't her problem—that she could stand up and pull off the cap and scream "*Here I am!*" anytime she wanted. But somehow, in her soul, she felt guilty, as if she were bringing this down on Reed.

". . . state attorneys are still reviewing proper protocol, but the constitution is clear, wherein the governor, the lieutenant governor, and the secretary of state are all rendered incapable of serving in the executive office, the attorney general will assume the governorship."

Maggie's head snapped up. What did he just say?

Three faces were on the screen now—the reporter and some pundits, sitting with plastered smiles. She recognized one of the pundits as House Majority Leader Tom Culley, and the realization made her want to wash her hands. Culley was a lot of things, but most of all, he was a politician—a greasy, back-room-dealing, baby-kissing politician.

"Well, James," Culley said, "let's not jump to conclusions. There is no reason to believe that Secretary Warner will be incapable or unwilling to assume office. We need to give him time to adjust and prepare a statement."

Senate Majority Leader Sally Frale broke in. "It's been more than fifteen hours since Governor Trousdale's disappearance, Tom. I think Secretary Warner has had ample time to step up to the plate, but he's not stepping. This state needs *leadership*. Not this afternoon, not tomorrow. Right now."

Maggie saw through the smoke of rhetoric and grandstanding. Secretary Warner and Majority Leader Culley shared the same political party, so, of course Culley would defend him. Frale represented the opposition, so it served her interests to make Secretary Warner—wherever the hell he was —the face of her enemy.

But where *was* Warner? Why hadn't he assumed office?

Maggie sat bolt upright.

Coulier. How could she have been so blind? Coulier was making a play for the executive office. Didn't he ask her, just days prior, for the lieutenant governorship? That would have placed him next in line after Maggie's death.

No. Coulier couldn't have known about the plot to assassinate her, could he? Was he actually involved with Gambit?

Reed's words echoed in her mind: *"Gambit wouldn't bring you down unless he controlled your successor."*

There was no way Coulier could be working for Gambit. She picked Coulier herself. How could Gambit have influenced that?

Maybe he didn't. Not at first, anyway. Maybe he got to Coulier after the fact and made him an offer he couldn't refuse—a chance to be the most powerful man in the state. Maggie remembered how Coulier had disappeared just prior to asking her to make him lieutenant governor. Then it was Coulier, not her, who thought of the press conference in New Orleans, after which Coulier had inexplicably disappeared again, only to reappear at the last moment to deliver that speech in her car. All that bullshit about bullies and justice and being a leader.

He went to meet with Gambit. Then he came back to ensure that I took the podium without admitting to anything, because he knew something was going to happen. He knew all along.

Maggie dropped a five-dollar bill on the table. It was time to go. Baton

Rouge was no longer safe for her, even if she returned. The only way to reclaim control was to find Gambit.

She hit speed dial on the phone and held it to her ear. Reed answered on the first ring.

"I've got it," he said. "I'm on my way out."

"Hurry. There've been more developments. I think Gambit has an inside man."

36

Reed slid the phone back into his pocket and hurried down the interior stairwell of the building. Behind him, inside the main offices of BANO, a secretary sat under her desk in petrified silence while her boss remained taped to a chair, an open pair of office scissors lying on the desk next to him.

BANO's office manager didn't require much convincing. While the brochures on his desk bragged about the discretion BANO offered their clients, the manager wasn't about to die for that discretion, and he blurted out the address before Reed could even draw blood with the scissors.

Reed slid through the exterior door and scanned the sidewalk for Maggie. She hurried from across the street, an alarm in her demeanor he hadn't seen before.

"You found it?"

Reed patted his pocket. "Another address, this one outside of town. A house, I think."

Maggie motioned down an alleyway leading away from the main street. "Let's get out of here. Something big is going down. I think my attorney general is involved now."

"We'll talk in the car," Reed said.

Reed took the lead, hurrying to the end of the alley and taking a right onto the adjoining backstreet. The BMW was parked another block away, hidden in a tiny lot behind a pizzeria. His heart rate quickened as the feeling of impending action—an altogether too familiar sensation—descended over his body.

I've got you now, Gambit. And I'm gonna burn you alive.

Reed rounded the next corner, and his entire world collapsed around him. The breath caught in his throat, and he unknowingly slid to a stop.

Banks stood on the opposing sidewalk twenty yards away, waiting for the crosswalk. There were two other women with her, and he recognized one of them as Little Bitch, one of Oliver's contractors. The other woman wore head-to-toe traditional Muslim dress, obscuring her face from view.

Reed barely processed any of that. Maggie slammed into him from behind, and he stumbled forward another foot, catching Banks's attention. She looked up, those bright blue eyes shining from across the street, instantly full of recognition, confliction, and pain, but not surprise.

Something between gut-wrenching agony and unbridled longing ripped through him. Cars whistled past, but their gaze didn't break. For a moment, he stared at her the way he did that first night in the Atlanta nightclub. He saw past her pain and the exhaustion that hung on her like a cloak, and he saw that fire he first fell in love with. Her nose was inexplicably swollen and purple, but even so, she was as beautiful in that moment as he had ever seen her.

"Reed . . ." Her lips moved, and she stepped forward as the crosswalk cleared.

And then Reed knew that Heaven and Earth wouldn't be able to stop Banks. She wasn't here because of her father, and she wasn't here because of her own anger. She was here because she believed that Reed could be saved, and as long as that door was open, she would never stop forcing her way through.

Reed turned on his heel and slid an arm behind Maggie's lower back, pulling her close. He kissed her on the mouth, long and slow, holding her as the moments dragged by like years. Maggie stiffened but didn't immediately recoil.

Reed released her and grabbed her hand, turning away from the crosswalk and hurrying down the sidewalk without a second glance. The two broke into a run, quickly disappearing into the tangle of tourists and business people.

The BMW sat unmolested where Reed had left it. He hit unlock and slid inside, his eyes burning as his stomach continued to convulse. The image of Banks's pleading face was burned into his mind—so deep and passionate, raw and unshielded, as though he could see into her very soul.

There was something in that look . . . something he couldn't be sure of. Was it the same thing he felt? Longing? Or did he only see what his heart wanted him to see?

Reed slammed the door, and Maggie settled in beside him. The car was quiet for a moment, and Reed looked out his window, fighting back the grief.

Maggie's voice was soft and unassuming. "Was that her?"

Reed nodded once, not caring that Maggie connected the dots. A single tear slipped past his guard and ran down his cheek. He gritted his teeth and wiped it away, then punched the start button.

"I'm sorry," he whispered. "I shouldn't—"

Maggie held up her hand. "I understand."

Reed put the car into gear, then powered out of the lot and turned out of the city. He focused his mind on the road ahead, but his heart kept interjecting that image of Banks—the way she stood, her hair gently cascading over her shoulders, silent and present, and so damn close.

Yet so far away.

"What now?" Maggie asked.

Reed focused on the road ahead as he fumbled in his pocket and pulled out the scratch paper.

"Do you recognize this address?"

Maggie unfolded the paper and sat up. "It's in Livingston Parish, right off Lake Maurepas. My god, it's just a mile from my family cabin."

Reed opened a bottle of water and drained half of it. "That's the official root address of ABC Consultants. I had to sift through about four LLCs to find it, but they were all managed by BANO, so it didn't take long."

"You think this is Gambit's headquarters?"

"No, I think it's probably just a property they own for registration purposes. Maybe a safe house."

"So, what's the plan?"

Reed twisted his hand around the wheel. "Before I say, I need to know how committed you are. My plans aren't usually legal. Or clean."

Maggie waved him off. "I'm tired of pulling punches. I need this SOB as bad as you do."

Reed finished the water, then cleared his throat. Before he could speak, the burner phone from Gambit erupted in his pocket. He shot her a sideways glance, then dug it out and hit the answer button.

"Yes?"

"*Reed Montgomery.*" The anger boiled out of Gambit's tone like a stream of lava. Reed had never heard him this emotional.

"What's up, Gambit?"

"You *know* what's up! The governor. She's still alive and missing. Or do you not watch the news?"

"You know you can't trust the news, Gambit." Reed kept his voice even. "The governor isn't dead, and she isn't missing, either. In fact, she's right here."

Reed hit the speaker button, and Maggie leaned toward the phone.

"Hello, pal."

Pregnant silence filled the car, punctuated only by a short inhale from Gambit.

Reed put the phone back into private mode and lifted it to his ear.

"Here's the thing, Gambit. I *really* hate being manipulated. It sets me off in a bad way. Just ask Oliver Enfield. Oh, wait. You can't."

Gambit's voice bubbled with restrained fury. "You think you're smart, but you're forgetting something, Montgomery. I still have your old man, and *I know where you are.*"

"Wrong. You know where some pothead with a backpack is because he's got your cheap-ass ankle monitor. But I'm not secretive. I'll tell you exactly where I am. I'm in your blind spot. And that's a hell of a place for a man like me to be. Are you ready to deal?"

Gambit's breath whistled again. Reed could feel the panic surging through the phone, but Gambit regained control of his tone.

"I don't think you're in a place to deal, Montgomery. David's mind is very fragile, you know. His psyche is on the edge of complete collapse. I'd hate to go there."

"So let's not go there. Let's make a trade . . . one prisoner for another."

"Trousdale is your prisoner?"

"Sure. Didn't you hear the desperation in her voice?"

Reed knew he was treading on thin ice, but then again, he didn't leave Gambit with many options.

"What do you have in mind?" Gambit asked.

"There's a lake west of downtown. Lake Maurepas. We'll meet on the south bank, in the woods. Don't bring those damn goons with you. Just bring my father, and I'll bring the governor."

"How do I know *you* won't bring goons?" Gambit snarled.

"Easy. I don't need goons."

Reed decided to push his luck.

"You *are* in New Orleans, aren't you? Doing some consulting or something?"

Gambit didn't respond, but there was a slight catch in his breath. Reed had hit pay dirt.

"I'm a loose cannon, Gambit, with a damn long range. Take my word for it—this is the best offer you're gonna get."

"Fine," Gambit snapped. "South bank of the lake. Ten p.m."

"Six p.m. I'm not giving you time to deploy an army."

Reed hung up before Gambit could answer, and he glanced at Maggie.

"Well, Governor, it's time to get muddy. Are you ready for that?"

Maggie folded her arms. "Been ready my whole life. Let's get this guy."

37

"Where's Wolfgang?" Lucy asked.

Banks frowned and glanced over her shoulder. The bustling streets of New Orleans surrounded them, crushing in with tourists and locals alike.

"He was just here. Did you see him, Kelly?"

Kelly shook her head, and Banks led the way down the sidewalk, rising on tiptoe to look for Wolfgang. They'd been in the city less than an hour, and already he'd given them the slip again.

She pressed ahead through the crowd, searching the faces of the men for any sign of their uncommitted male associate. Wolfgang was nowhere to be seen, and Banks stopped at an intersection, brushing hair out of her face and shrugging.

"I don't see him."

Kelly grumbled something about the worthlessness of the male species, and Banks jammed her hands into her pockets, watching the cars flash past as she waited for the crosswalk to open.

Then she saw Reed.

He caught her gaze from the far side of the intersection as he barreled down the sidewalk toward her. She recognized his form long before she saw his features—tall and broad, with the same iron glint in his eyes that told her Reed Montgomery was yet again at war.

A surge of hope flooded Banks's heart, and she started to lift one hand, but the glint in his eyes faded, collapsing in sparks as their gazes met. A woman was with Reed, dressed in a Saints T-shirt with an LSU cap jammed over dirty-blonde hair. She stood next to Reed, her posture braced for flight as she glanced nervously around the intersection. Cars whistled by in the space between Reed and Banks, and all of a sudden, overwhelming longing surged through her.

She wanted to run, to rush between the cars and across the street and throw herself at him, to pull him in and hold him close and find out why the hell he ever left her. The longing intensified when she saw the same feelings reflected back at her. She was certain of it.

The moments dragged by in slow motion before the light changed and the cars squeaked to a halt, leaving the crosswalk open. Banks took one shuddering half step forward, her mind swimming.

And then something hard and unfeeling and painful crossed over his face. He turned away and scooped up the woman, kissing her just like he kissed Banks that first night in the parking garage in Atlanta.

The world collapsed around her. Banks's half step fell short, and she stumbled into the street as tears spilled down her face. Reed turned and ran without a second glance, towing the woman along with him. Despair crashed in on Banks, ripping through her mind, when she felt strong hands on her arms, pulling her back onto the sidewalk as turning cars rushed by.

Banks's vision blurred, and Lucy pulled her away from the sidewalk as Kelly broke into a run across the street, sliding between honking horns and pursuing Reed. Banks slid onto a park bench, and Lucy settled down beside her, pulling her close.

"It's okay, sweetie," Lucy whispered as Banks began to sob.

"Something's wrong," Banks mumbled. "It's not what it looks like."

Lucy didn't reply, but she ran a soft hand through Banks's hair and rocked her as Banks covered her face with both hands and tried to erase the image of that kiss from her mind.

Kelly and Wolfgang appeared at the same time, ten minutes later. Banks sat on the bench with mascara running down her face, but she wasn't crying anymore. Lucy sipped on a bottle of water with cold green eyes staring across the street.

"I lost him," Kelly said. "He had a car. Black BMW, local plates."

Lucy glanced at Banks, who looked broken, like a woman run through a car crusher. For a moment, Lucy tried to imagine what Banks felt, but it was difficult. She'd never been in love, herself. Not since she watched her father burn alive in the mangled wreck of his Indy car. Since that day, Lucy found it easier to suppress all feelings of positive emotions and embrace only the burning fire that drove her along to her next kill—her next balancing of the scales.

But the pain in Banks's face . . . she understood that. Maybe not for the same reasons, but certainly in an abstract way. It was the pain of loss, betrayal, and confusion.

"What do you mean, *you lost him*?" Wolfgang panted. "Reed was *here*?"

"Unfortunately," Lucy said.

Wolfgang ran a hand through his hair, and the four of them were silent for a moment.

Kelly spat into the grass.

"I'm going to gut him like a dog."

Banks's voice cracked with sudden anger. "Shut up!" She bolted to her feet and delivered a rabbit punch to Kelly's sternum.

Kelly stumbled back, choking for air as Banks followed up the punch with another shove, hurling the shorter woman into the grass.

"I've had *enough* of you, you bitter, nasty, hateful woman!"

Kelly sat on the grass, sprawled backward. The headdress rippled over her ragged breaths, and tears stained it a darker shade of black.

Banks's hands shook as she jabbed a finger at Kelly.

"I don't know what that was about, but it wasn't what it looked like. You hear me?"

Lucy stood and grabbed Banks by the hand. "Calm down. You're drawing attention."

Banks waved Kelly away with a disgusted flick of her wrist and sat down again.

Kelly picked herself up and straightened the burka.

"You're not the only one he's hurt, you know!"

Lucy held up a finger. "She's right. You need to calm down." She turned to Wolfgang.

"Where the hell did you go? We lost you on the street."

Wolfgang twisted his neck until it popped, then slumped forward. "There was a commotion. I followed an instinct. Don't worry about it."

"Don't worry about it? Listen, hotshot. I'm very worried about it because I still don't trust you. What did you find?"

Wolfgang chewed his lip.

"I don't think I'm ready to—"

"No more bullshit!" Banks stood up and jabbed a finger in Wolfgang's face. "I'm sick and tired of the games. This is *my* mission. You're here because I *invited you*. Get with the program, or get the hell out!"

Wolfgang deflected the jabbing finger with his forearm and turned to Lucy.

Before Lucy could intervene, Banks started shouting again.

"Don't look at her! You work for *me*. What did you find?"

Again, Wolfgang hesitated, then sighed and motioned toward the parking lot where they left the Mercedes.

"Not here," Wolfgang said. "We've drawn enough attention."

Banks stomped after him. Lucy sighed and followed after her as Kelly trailed them.

When they were back inside the luxury coupe, Banks turned to Wolfgang.

"All right, spit it out."

Wolfgang rubbed his temples as if he were fighting back a headache or just restraining himself.

"There's a building down the street. Some kind of business registration service. Reed was there, I guess, because the usual chaos marked his path. A guy was taped up in a chair, and I freed him and asked him what happened. He said a big guy came in and wanted an address, so I got the address. It's a house or something outside of town."

Banks frowned. "What does that mean?"

Nobody answered, and she slammed her hand against the dash. "I said, *what does that mean?*"

"It means he's hunting!" In an uncharacteristic snap that caused the three women to stiffen, Wolfgang said, "It means he's hunting!" He twisted to face them, his knuckles turning white around the wheel.

"I don't know what he's after, but it isn't the governor. Reed's running somebody or something to ground."

"What is it?" Lucy said.

Wolfgang looked away. "How should I know? Do I look psychic?"

"You *should* know," she said, "because you talked to Reed, as we've already established. You're still bullshitting us, Wolf."

Lucy wasn't actually sure if Wolfgang knew or not, but she still had the uneasy feeling that there was more to the story. Wolfgang was shielding something, or somebody, and she would have much preferred to dig out the truth without Banks and Kelly present. But that wasn't going to happen.

Wolfgang rubbed his temples again.

"Wolf?" Banks pressed. "What do you know?"

"David Montgomery," Wolfgang said softly.

Lucy frowned at the name, but Banks seemed to recognize it.

"They have him, don't they?" Banks asked.

Wolfgang massaged his temples and nodded.

"Who's David Montgomery?" Lucy asked.

"His father," Kelly said.

"He asked you to get rid of me, didn't he?" Banks asked, her voice softer now.

Wolfgang nodded again.

Banks sat quiet for a moment, then buckled her seatbelt. "Drive."

Wolfgang looked up. "What?"

"Drive!"

"Where?"

"To that address, genius. If Reed is looking for David, we're going to help."

Wolfgang shook his head and lifted a finger. "You see, this is exactly why I won't tell you stuff. Whatever Reed is mixed up in, you can bet it's gonna be bloody. If these people have his father, they're not gonna give him up easily. There will be serious fireworks."

"Fine." Banks unbuckled herself. "I'll do it."

She reached for the door handle, but Wolfgang grabbed her arm. "You don't have the address!"

"Nope, but I have a pistol, and I know there's a guy down the street who has the address."

Wolfgang turned to Lucy, his grip still on Banks's arm. Lucy sighed and motioned for him to release her.

Banks pivoted in the seat to face the group.

"I don't care what you saw on the street just now. Reed is in trouble and backed into a corner. He owes me answers as much as any of you, and . . ."

Her voice cracked, and she swallowed. "And I'm not letting this go. I'm *going* to that house. Are you coming or not?"

Lucy and Wolfgang exchanged another look, but there was nothing left to be said. Banks was impossible.

Wolfgang threw up his hands, his old sarcasm returning like a sudden burst of fireworks.

"Fine! Geez. *Women* . . . You guys are a royal, never-ending pain in the neck." He punched the start button, and the big German engine roared to life. "The address is outside of town, near some lake. We'll be there by nightfall."

38

Gambit had never felt panic like the kind of mad, animalistic fear that gripped him now. For almost five years he played Aiden's dangerous game, working for a network of criminal organizations that orbited around a single, deadly operation. It was profitable—insanely so—but more than that, it gave Gambit a purpose. He was a man of power, a man of resources. It made him feel like a puppet master working behind the curtain, pulling the strings, and making people dance like madmen.

It didn't bother him that Aiden stood behind him, pulling his own strings. The drug of control, influence, and power was something Gambit had been addicted to since grade school, always rising to the top, taking the lead, and calling the shots.

He couldn't quit; he never had the chance. Being a manipulator brought him to life like nothing else, and Gambit had tried plenty of real drugs in search of a substitute that offered less potential to destroy his life. He'd never found one, which left him here in the precarious position of being the king of a glass castle, only a blow away from shattering.

And yet, he never believed that would happen. Wasn't he in control?

Couldn't he manipulate his way into more and more power until he finally bit the dust?

That was the plan, but in this moment, all the manipulations felt worthless. Gambit made a critical, deadly error. He underestimated somebody, overestimated his influence over that individual, and now he was backed into a corner.

Reed Montgomery was off the leash.

Gambit hurried down a flight of stairs and into the dank basement of his temporary New Orleans operation center. David was in a chair in a corner but not tied up; he didn't need to be. In spite of what Gambit told Reed, David was far from competent. His brain was fried harder than an egg on a flatiron, and there was no hope of restoring it. Sure, from time to time, there were glimpses of humanity that crossed behind David's glassy eyes, helped along by a hint of stimulating narcotic. Reed had been witness to that hint of humanity in the woods of North Alabama, and he fell for it hook, line, and sinker. It was the perfect manipulation . . . until it wasn't.

Gambit snapped his fingers at the two goons lounging in the background, reading porn mags and smoking cigarettes.

"On your feet!" he growled. "We have to move."

They hauled themselves up, dropping the smokes on the concrete and stomping them out. Handguns glistened from their belts, along with combat knives and extra magazines. These guys weren't exactly spec ops soldiers, but Gambit was confident in their ability and absolute willingness to gun down anybody who got in their way.

That was enough. He hoped.

The phone in his pocket vibrated, and that animalistic fear in his stomach erupted into a hurricane. Gambit checked the caller ID, and his worst terror was confirmed. It was Aiden.

He hesitated only a moment, then hit the answer button. As much as he wanted to crush the phone under his shoe and run for the hills, he knew better. There was no place on this planet that he could hide from Aiden. Now, his only hope was to somehow turn this situation on its head—to bury Governor Trousdale and Reed Montgomery with her.

"Yes?"

"Explain." Aiden's single word was laced with a calm menace.

Gambit didn't have to ask what it was that Aiden wanted explained, and he didn't dare embellish the details or pad the reality.

"Montgomery is out of control. Trousdale is still alive. Montgomery has her, and he's demanding an exchange for David."

"Your plan?" Aiden's voice was barbed with enough edge to slice through a block wall.

"I'm setting him up near the lake. He won't make it out alive."

"Good. Kill David and the governor, also."

Gambit swallowed. "Yes, sir. I will."

"I don't have to remind you what's at stake here. If any of the three survive the night, I recommend that *you do not*."

An icy claw sank into Gambit's soul, digging in and clutching him in the deepest parts of his being. It was fear and panic and desperate hope all balled into one until he couldn't tell the difference between the three.

Two Montgomerys and one Trousdale. Either they all had to die . . . or he did.

The phone clicked off before Gambit could say anything more, and he motioned to his men. "Move him! Into the van, now. Take all your combat gear."

As the two goons began to haul David up the stairs, Gambit selected another phone contact and hit the dial button. The line connected on the third ring.

"Gordon, it's Gambit. I'm headed your way. We need the house."

39

Lake Maurepas
Livingston Parish, Louisiana

The last three days faded into a blur for Gordon. The little house by the lake had processed six clients in total—most of them were there for the same raven-haired Scandinavian girl that Mr. Porsche had flown all the way from Australia to "experience." The girl was a hot commodity, but Gordon would have to rest or retire her soon. Some of the clients were more violent than others, leaving bruises or even cuts. Of course, Gordon charged them extra for that, but each blemish reduced the girl's value. At some point, there would be a decision to make: give the girl to a particularly brutal, even murderous client, and cash out before burying her body in the swamp, or let her recover for a couple weeks before putting her back on his dark web homepage for a lower price and then repeating the cycle.

The decision would be based entirely on supply. If another fresh, clean girl was available, he'd bury the Scandinavian without a second thought, just like he had so many girls before her.

Gordon unbuttoned his shirt and let it hang open over his considerable gut as he waddled across the kitchen to fix a sandwich. Two clients were downstairs in the hotel rooms—a Japanese guy with the Scandinavian, and some backwoods redneck from Arkansas with a blonde girl a couple years older. The redneck was rough; Gordon doubted the blonde would survive. And that was okay because he already knew the redneck could pay. The blonde had been around almost a month anyway.

Gordon cracked a beer open and slurped down half of it before indulging in a deep burp. Neither of the clients downstairs were the video-tape kind; they were ordinary. Move them in, deliver their experience, and cut them loose. Gordon's boss was unlikely to be pleased with so many of these "ordinary" clients, as they drastically increased the overall risk of the operation. But Gordon was making a killing, and what his boss didn't know wouldn't hurt him.

Sid wandered into the kitchen, his dark eyes darting from one end of the room to the other with restless unease. Sid was a rodent, a creature of dark alleys and small, grimy places. But like a rodent, Sid possessed a remarkable instinct for survival, and that was the chief reason Gordon kept him around.

"We need to slow down," Sid whined. "This makes six clients in a week. You'll spoil the product."

Gordon burped and shrugged. "I can get more."

"What if the boss finds out?"

"I'll worry about the boss. You just do what you do . . . facilitate. Don't forget, you're getting a big commission this week."

Sid nodded a couple times, then he wandered out of the room again.

Gordon finished his beer and was about to lay out bread for another sandwich when a dull buzz erupted in his pocket. His heart rate quickened, and he snatched the phone out. A pop-up message on the screen read "Call."

That message was only displayed when a call rang in through his secure landline, and only one person ever called that line: the boss.

Gordon dropped the bread and hustled into the hallway, his breath whistling in ragged heaves between steps. He checked over his shoulder, then opened the hidden panel beneath the stairwell to the second floor, and slid inside.

A red light blinked next to the phone on the desk, but there was no ring.

Gordon settled into his desk chair and struggled to catch his breath, then scooped up the phone and held it to his ear.

"What's up, boss?"

"Gordon, it's Gambit."

There was a stress level in his tone that Gordon had never heard before. It was almost a panic.

"I'm headed your way," Gambit continued. "We need the house."

Fresh sweat broke out over Gordon's forehead.

"Right now?"

"Did you not hear me? *I'm headed your way.*"

Gordon's mind raced. He wasn't supposed to have clients at the house right then, and Gambit knew that. These clients were purely extracurricular, off the books. Gambit, and whoever Gambit worked for, wasn't getting a cut off of them. Gordon and Sid split the profits 70/30, which was fine—they'd done it many times before. But they'd never been caught.

"I just mean . . ." Gordon hesitated. "It doesn't seem safe, boss. We gotta keep this place a secret, you know?"

"I'll worry about that, you pig," Gambit snarled. "Trust me, anybody coming to that house tonight won't be alive to talk about it tomorrow."

The phone trembled in Gordon's clammy hands, and he started to speak again. But if he told Gambit the truth now, there was no reason why Gambit wouldn't replace him the following day, or worse, eliminate him.

No, he couldn't tell Gambit. He had to handle this.

"Okay, boss. When will you be here?"

"Thirty minutes."

The phone clicked off, and Gordon lumbered to his feet, crashing through the paneled door.

"Sid!" he shouted. "Sid, get up here!"

Sid appeared out of the shadows of the basement stairwell, his rodent eyes flashing in the dim light.

"What is it?" he whined.

"The boss is on the way. We've got to clean things up."

"Clean things up? What do you mean? *Kick them out?*"

"No." Gordon swabbed sweat off his head as he chewed on his lip a moment. "Move the redneck upstairs. We've got a white guy booked for next week—one of the boss's clients. We'll tell the boss he came early."

"But what about the other client?"

"Tell the Japanese guy we're treating him to an extra hour, then bar off the basement. We'll tell the boss there's been a leak downstairs and that we're hosting clients upstairs."

Sid tore at his greasy hair with both hands. "What if the boss hears something? What if the Japanese guy finishes early?"

Gordon pushed Sid toward the basement door. "You stay down there. If the Japanese guy becomes a problem, kill him."

40

Reed lay prone in the damp Louisiana dirt, nestled just behind a rotting log, and squinted through the scope of the Springfield. Two hundred yards away, the house by the lake sat in almost total darkness as the sun vanished behind the leafless trees. A yellow glow shone through windows on the second floor, and Reed could see the shadows of at least three people, but he couldn't make out faces.

The front of the house faced a gentle slope that led to the lakeshore, and the rear faced a small gravel parking lot with trees all around.

Reed pivoted the crosshairs across the front porch of the home. He took note of the absence of furniture or decorations at the front door, then swung the scope to the back of the house, where a late-model Range Rover and a couple European sedans were parked.

Reed drew a breath and repeated the sweep, searching for signs of Gambit, his goons, or David Montgomery. So far, there was nothing.

"You told him to meet us at the south bank," Maggie whispered as she lay beside him, peering through a pair of binoculars. "What makes you so sure he'll use this house?"

The house sat over two miles off the primary blacktop that served this part of the parish. It took almost an hour to find, even with the aid of the address Reed had pulled from the terrified office manager of BANO earlier that day.

"This house wasn't meant to be found," Reed whispered. "Whatever's going on here, it's linked to Gambit via his chain of shell companies. In fact, this house is owned by a shell company—some distant cousin of ABC Consultants. This place is a key part of Gambit's operation."

"Right," Maggie whispered. "So you'd think he'd want to isolate us from that. Keep us as far away as possible."

Reed nodded, still surveying the house with the scope, his finger resting just above the trigger guard. "That's why I kept the time frame so short. Gambit will need reinforcements if he plans to gun us down, which I'm sure he does. I didn't give him time to find any, so he'll have to use whatever resources he has close to hand. This house is close to hand."

"So, he shows up . . . What then?"

Reed wiped sweat from his forehead, momentarily marveling that he was sweating at all this late in the year.

"Once he arrives, I'll work to eliminate the primary guards. With luck, we can isolate my father while remaining at a distance. Then we'll move in."

Maggie nodded and turned toward him.

"Reed."

He looked away from the rifle, meeting her gaze. "What?"

"I'll need Gambit for my investigation. Take him out of the fight, but *don't kill him*. Are we clear?"

Reed chewed his lip, searching the dark depths of Maggie's iron stare for a moment, where he saw fire, rage, and a tinge of hatred. This was Louisiana's governor, and Gambit was Louisiana's enemy. Muddy Maggie was at war.

He grunted, then settled behind the scope. Gambit wasn't the end of this war—Aiden Phillips, Gambit's boss, was. If Maggie wanted Gambit, that was fine with him.

He shut his left eye and resumed surveillance of the house. It was already six o'clock, with only a half hour standing between them and their scheduled appointment with Gambit. For better or for worse, something was about to happen.

"I have movement!" Maggie hissed.

Reed used his peripheral vision to identify which direction she was looking in, then spun the rifle to follow her line of sight. He gently disengaged the safety with a flick of his index finger.

Bingo.

A dark shape moved toward the house from the far side of the driveway, maybe two hundred fifty yards out and closing.

"There's another," Maggie whispered.

"I see it," Reed confirmed, sliding the crosshairs from the first dark figure to the second, then a third, and then a fourth, each moving through the trees and toward the house.

"Can you make out faces?" Reed asked.

Maggie didn't reply, so he opened his left eye, using his peripheral vision to check on her. She slowly lowered the binoculars from her line of sight and shot him a sideways glance.

Reed redirected his gaze through the optic and zoomed in, magnifying the crosshairs over the face of the lead individual. As the clouds parted in the dark sky and the moon shone down from overhead, his heart leapt into his throat.

Banks.

Banks crept through the trees, taking care to place each foot on the most solid section of ground she could find as she worked her way toward the house. The Smith & Wesson .38 from T-Rex's van was tucked into her waistband, and the bandolier of 20-gauge shells hung across her chest while the shotgun rode in a two-handed grip, ready for action.

"Slow up," Lucy whispered. "You're making too much noise."

The group stopped a couple hundred yards from the house, and they knelt behind the low brush blocking their path. Other than the whistle of Kelly's obstructed breathing, they remained quiet. Banks cast a glance around her small band of warriors, although calling them *warriors* was a stretch. Kelly was now dressed in black pants and boots but still wore the headdress that covered everything but her vision. In her skintight leather bodysuit, Lucy had both swords strapped to her sides and two long knives fitted to sheaths across her abs.

Wolfgang brought up the rear, dressed as he always was in leather evening shoes, grey pants, and his peacoat—never mind the fact that it was over eighty degrees in the swamp. He carried an M4 assault rifle equipped with a red dot sight, a high-capacity drum magazine, and a flashlight. Of the four of them, he was by far the best equipped, yet Banks felt as though he was the least committed.

"Okay," Banks hissed. "Here's what we're gonna do—"

Lucy held up a finger. "If I may, sweetie, this is more my area of expertise than yours."

Banks hesitated, momentarily perturbed that Lucy had usurped control of the operation, but she acquiesced. Lucy was, in fact, an actual assassin who probably knew all kinds of things about tactics and sneaking. Now that the four were finally at the house, Banks was less fearful of the operation being canceled.

Lucy squatted in the dirt and raised a night-vision monocular to her right eye—provided courtesy of Wolfgang. She scanned the house, then lowered the monocular.

"Okay, I'm not seeing any guards. We have no reason to think Reed is inside, but before we start World War Three, we really need some solid intel. Agreed?"

Wolfgang and Banks nodded, and Kelly continued to pretend that she was the only person on the planet.

"Right," Lucy continued. "So let's close in to about fifty yards. Wolf, you'll set up there and provide cover fire, if necessary. Banks and Kelly, you'll provide perimeter support to block any attempted escapees. I'll make an intrusion into the house and scope out the situation."

"I want to go," Banks hissed.

Lucy shook her head.

"No, honey. Don't be offended, but you're much too loud. This is my specialty. Trust me, if shit goes down, you'll see some action."

Banks opened her mouth to offer further protest, but Kelly held up her fist, and they all crouched lower into the undergrowth.

Tires crunched against the gravel driveway only a moment before the bright gleam of headlights broke through the trees.

Wolfgang raised the M4, his finger stiff next to the trigger guard as he traced the progress of the vehicle with the red dot sight. Banks could see it now—a bulky SUV, black with dark windows, aggressively rolling up the driveway and crashing through mud puddles.

It wasn't Reed, she knew that. Reed would never drive that way, making so much noise and remaining so exposed. Whoever it was, they were familiar with this place and possibly even owned it.

The SUV slid to a stop adjacent to the back steps of the house, and the engine cut off. A beefy man with bulky arms stepped out of the driver seat, followed by another from the passenger seat, both men armed with short-ened assault weapons. They circled to the back of the SUV and opened the hatch while a third man slid out of the back seat. Tall and trim, he was dressed in a three-piece suit and wore sunglasses, despite the darkness.

The first two ducked into the back of the SUV and hauled out a fourth figure—another man, gagged, and bound hand and foot. His body was limp, and his head rolled on a loose neck, but he stood on his own two feet after being hauled out of the SUV.

"Night vision," Wolfgang said.

Lucy handed him the monocular.

"That's David Montgomery," Wolfgang whispered.

"Are you sure?" Lucy asked.

Wolfgang nodded, following the progress of the four men as they ascended the steps and ducked inside the house. "Positive. I reviewed his prison file. Plus, he looks just like Reed."

Wolfgang lowered the night vision and turned back to the three women.

Lucy bit her lip and continued to stare at the house, then pivoted to the group.

"We should call this off. If David is inside that house and there's even a chance that Reed knows about it, he's about to light this place up."

"I agree," Wolfgang said quickly.

Banks stood up, fire shooting through her veins. "Are you kidding me? You're all a bunch of bitches! If they've got Reed's father, we need to rescue him!"

Lucy grabbed Banks's hand and pulled her back into the brush. "Sweetie, nobody here is scared of a fight. But we've been in enough of them to know that tactics and patience win the war, not passion. We need to consider—"

A man's shout broke out from the house, followed by the sound of breaking glass.

"What do you *mean* the client came early?"

"Please! Don't hurt me, boss!" cried another voice. "He's upstairs, okay? I wanted to tell you—"

A gunshot rang out, sharp and clear, followed by a meaty thud.

"Search the house! Throw the client in a cell, and get rid of the girls."

Banks leapt to her feet, already running toward the back door. She didn't care if the others followed her, and she didn't care who was inside. This was the man she had been hunting—maybe the man who killed her father. He was killing again, right now, and she wasn't about to watch it happen.

41

Reed watched as the Tahoe crashed toward the house and slid to a stop, leaving its passenger side fully exposed to his rifle. The windows were tinted, preventing him from making out the faces of anybody inside, but he slipped his finger onto the trigger and held his breath as the doors flew open.

Two big men, with assault rifles swinging from one-point slings, stepped out first. He recognized them as Gambit's personal goons. The driver disappeared on the far side of the vehicle, but the second guy remained visible as he circled to the back of the Tahoe and threw open the hatch.

Reed could've dropped him with a press of the trigger. At two hundred yards, it would've been as easy as taking out soda cans with a BB gun, but if he fired now, the other man would have time to respond, and he still didn't know where David or Gambit were.

He could see a slight glint of light in the passenger side rear window. Maybe Gambit was climbing out the other side. The goon's partner joined him at the rear of the SUV, and they bent over, momentarily obscuring his shot as they dragged somebody out.

It was David, no doubt about it. His father pivoted on his feet, now obstructing his view of the goons. David stood unassisted, but his head lolled downward, his chin riding against his chest.

Rage surged through Reed's mind, and he pivoted the rifle, searching for a target.

"Do you still have Banks?" he said.

"Negative," Maggie said. "I lost them in the brush."

The men hauled David to the far side of the SUV, and for a moment, they all faded from view. Reed caught flashes of arms and shoulders as they passed into the house, but the bulk of the SUV still blocked a clean shot.

The screen door smacked shut, and Reed cursed. He pivoted the scope across the front of the house, checking each window, searching for a shot. Through the blinds, he could see the silhouettes of occupants inside, but he couldn't be sure which ones were targets and which one was David.

"We need them outside," he said.

"It's a quarter to six," Maggie said. "He'll have to call us soon."

A commotion broke out from the house, and Reed snapped the rifle back to the windows.

"Are you sure she's not in there?" Reed said.

"I just saw her! Nine o'clock, maybe seventy yards from the house. She's ducked back into the brush now."

Reed cursed every flavor of bad luck that was rapidly taking control of his night. How the hell had Banks found this place? The only possible explanation was that she somehow discovered the address, probably the same way that he had. Maybe Wolfgang or Little Bitch helped her. Both were smart enough to get it done, but *why* were they helping her? Why were any of them there?

More screams, and a gunshot ripped through the night as loud and sudden as a nuclear blast. Another chorus of shots, and Reed laid his finger on the trigger again.

Maggie put a hand on his arm.

"Wait!" she snapped, still staring into the binoculars. "She's running!"

"What do you mean *she's running*?"

"She's running toward the house. I think she's got a gun. Wait! The others are following."

Reed took his finger off the trigger and set the crosshairs over Banks's progress. He could see her blonde hair waving in the breeze as she dashed toward the house with what appeared to be a shotgun cradled in her arms. Little Bitch followed, moving like a wraith with a sword in each hand. Just behind them was the third woman in the burka he'd seen earlier that day in New Orleans.

She no longer wore the full-body dress but was clothed in tight black pants and a T-shirt, with a black headdress obscuring her face. Something about her silhouette was familiar—hauntingly so—but he couldn't place it.

Then he saw Wolfgang moving behind the others and to the left, taking up a position behind a fallen log. He carried an M4 assault rifle with a one-hundred-round drum magazine, and only a moment after falling behind the log, he opened fire on the house.

As she broke into a run, Banks didn't give a damn about the shouts from Lucy and Wolfgang. The bandolier slapped against her stomach and she slammed the pump action of the shotgun back and then forward, ramming a load of buckshot into the chamber. Brush and mud slapped and splashed against her legs, and she almost fell, her breath coming in heavy bursts punctuated by the pounding of her heart.

"Wolf, cover fire!" Lucy shouted from a couple yards behind. The command was followed only a moment later by the *sheenk* sounds of Lucy's twin blades clearing their respective scabbards, and then the clicking of Kelly chambering her pistol.

They were with her. The thought sent a fresh surge of adrenaline into Banks's body, and she cleared a log, throwing herself forward onto the gravel of the parking lot as the sharp snarl of Wolfgang's automatic rifle opened up on the house.

Bullets slammed into the roof as Wolfgang's raking fire ripped through the trees. Reed pivoted the rifle to follow the progress of the three women. Banks ran with the lumbering ambition of somebody who rarely ran but wouldn't be stopped by hell or high water. Just behind her, Little Bitch and the woman in the burka kept pace, both armed, both ready for war.

"These are your friends?" Maggie said.

"I don't know who they are!" Reed snapped as another swath of gunfire ripped over the heads of the three running women and blasted the back side of the house.

Wolfgang was smart, placing his shots at sections of the house unlikely to result in any unwanted casualties but certain to make everybody inside think twice about sticking their heads out long enough to return fire.

"Reed, front door!" Maggie said.

Reed pivoted the rifle just in time to catch the front door bursting open as David Montgomery was shoved out. Gambit followed close behind, a nickel-plated revolver clutched in one hand and jammed against David's temple as Gambit's panicked eyes darted through the trees, his face flooded with terror. The two goons followed just behind Gambit, pushing each other forward with the muzzles of the assault weapons sweeping the forest around them.

"Cover your ears!" Reed shouted. He swung the rifle to the left, his finger already depressing the trigger as the crosshairs passed across the sternum of the left-hand goon. The Springfield boomed like a cannon, spitting a 165-grain bullet out of the muzzle at over 2,800 feet per second. The projectile made impact before the goon even heard the shot, shattering his chest and blowing out his spine as he toppled to the ground.

Reed swung to the right, searching for the second target, but Gambit's other goon was better trained than Reed anticipated. The big man hit the dirt and opened fire at the same time, launching a string of automatic gunfire around them. Reed grabbed Maggie, and the two of them hurtled to the ground as a few close shots zipped through the air only inches over their heads.

"Stay down!" Reed barked, grabbing the fallen rifle and maneuvering to the far edge of the log for a follow-up shot. Another burst of gunfire shredded the trees and sent a shower of bark and dead limbs raining over them as he squinted into the scope.

Gambit had disappeared into the forest where the edge of the lake lapped against the mud. Reed took a quick shot at the second goon as the big man followed his boss into the woods, but the bullet smacked into the trunk of a tree, missing by mere inches.

"Damn!" Reed searched for another target as more commotion rose from the house, but he no longer cared about that. David Montgomery was somewhere out there, and he had to find him.

Reed jerked himself to his feet and started to step over the log, rifle in hand. He heard other sounds that gave him pause—a grumbling and coughing, followed by a ripping roar.

It was a boat engine.

He yanked the scope back to his eye and searched the woods at the far side of the yard. Everything was drenched in shadow, and he couldn't make out any specifics at the lake edge, but the motor sound was clear and growing louder as the boat gained speed and moved away from the bank.

"He's got a boat!" Reed snarled, starting forward again.

Maggie caught his shirt, pulling him back.

"Wait! You'll never catch him that way. I know where another boat is."

42

Banks planted her boot into the back door of the house, knocking it open with a crash and charging through with no regard for what lay on the other side. The light blinded her momentarily, and she heard a click to her right as she blinked into focus.

She saw the man lying on the floor a moment too late. His giant belly rested on his thighs, and blood seeped from a bullet hole just above his navel. His face was washed white in agony, but he held a snub-nose revolver and pointed it toward Banks, his finger wrapping around the trigger.

Lucy's sword flashed like a silver bullet, flicking downward and slicing through the fat man's forearm. Both his hand and the pistol dropped to the floor with a thud, but he didn't have time to scream. Lucy's second blade circled down from the left, slicing into his neck and decapitating him effortlessly.

Banks's stomach convulsed, but she was too blinded by adrenaline to stop. A female's scream broke out from down the hallway, and she turned in that direction.

"Check upstairs," Lucy shouted. "We'll take this floor!"

Banks burst down the hallway and found herself confronted by a narrow stairway that led upward toward the pain-filled screams. The closer Banks drew to their source, the younger the screams sounded. Like a child.

"No! Please! *Help me!*"

Banks took the steps two at a time, leaping to the top and spinning to the left. The two rooms were both shut and dead-bolted from the outside.

"Please, don't!"

Banks flicked the dead bolt open to the second room and kicked the door open, her vision once again flooded with light.

A half-naked girl was tied to the bed, blood running from long lacerations in her exposed stomach, and her eyes searched the ceiling as she continued to scream for help.

Standing over her was a shirtless white man with a dirty beard and Arian tattoos covering his torso. Music blared so loudly from his earbuds that Banks could hear it from across the room. He raised a folded leather belt over one shoulder and peered down at the girl with wicked delight, but that glint rapidly faded into fear as he turned toward the door.

Banks processed the scene in a split second, her focus landing first on the girl, then the man, then the belt. She raised the shotgun and clamped her left eye shut, the muzzle of the weapon hovering over his pelvis.

Panic filled his eyes as he shouted and held up a hand. Banks pulled the trigger. The gun belched fire into the room, sending a load of buckshot ripping through the air and slicing into the man's left hip. He flipped sideways off the bed, a horrible howl ripping from his throat as Banks circled the bed and pumped another shell into the chamber. Blinded with tears and rage, her blood pumped so hard and hot that she felt as though her body was burning from the inside out.

The man lay on the floor, writhing in blood as he clawed at his obliterated hip.

"No! Please!" he screamed.

Banks lowered the muzzle until it hovered only inches from his face, and she jerked the trigger.

Lucy and Kelly cleared the bottom floor of the house and progressed into the darkened stairwell that led to the basement. From overhead, Lucy heard screams, followed by the boom of Banks's shotgun—once, then a second time, back-to-back. She started to turn, but Kelly shoved her forward.

"Move, ninja girl. This isn't over."

Lucy led the way into the stairwell as they both adjusted to the darkness. The boards squeaked under their feet, and then Lucy's toe caught on something hard and unmoving. She stumbled forward, struggling to break her fall as one of her swords clattered to the floor. A gunshot rang out inches from her ear, sending a cracking sound ripping through her skull like a tidal wave.

"Duck!" Kelly snapped.

Lucy stumbled and tried to face her attacker, but Kelly was quicker. A short, rat-like man huddled in the shadows two steps down the stairwell, a handgun clamped in his shaking hand as his beady eyes glared upward.

Kelly rushed forward and knocked the gun out of the way. Her left forearm swung upward, catching the rat-man by the throat and pinning him against the wall. Then she rammed the muzzle of her pistol against his gut and fired three times while staring straight into his eyes.

The body collapsed to the floor, and Kelly kicked the fallen sword out of the way as she continued down the steps. Lucy scooped up her weapon and followed, casting a glimpse at the rodent man to make sure he was down.

At the bottom of the stairs was an unlocked door, and Kelly yanked it open while flicking a light switch with her left hand.

At the end of the short hallway, she saw an open steel door and two open hotel-style doors on either side. Kelly led with her gun as Lucy followed, clearing first the left-hand room before moving to the right. Kelly froze in the entrance of the second door, the pistol hovering at eye-level.

Lucy caught up, peering over her shoulder and immediately realizing why Kelly stopped.

Sitting on a king-size bed, surrounded by tangled sheets, was a Japanese man with a small handgun clamped in his hand. The muzzle of the weapon was pressed against the temple of a small girl—no older than twelve, Lucy guessed—with raven hair and crystal blue eyes. She was naked and curled into a ball to cover herself.

"One more step, and I blow her brains out!" the Japanese man snarled.

Kelly's fingers turned white around the pistol, but she didn't pull the trigger.

"Put down the gun!" the man yelled.

"Not a chance," Kelly said. "You're dying tonight, one way or another."

He sniffed derisively. "You don't know who I am, do you? Money, power . . . these things mean nothing to me. They are like water in the hand, flowing—"

Kelly twitched to the left, exposing a slit between her right side and the doorjamb. It was enough. One of the two long knives cleared the sheath with a whispered whir, only a millisecond before Lucy flicked it forward. It whistled through the space and found its home in the Japanese man's right elbow, immediately disabling his arm as Kelly rushed forward. He fell backward with a scream, struggling to fire his gun, but his arm convulsed uselessly. The girl shrieked and pulled away as Lucy ran forward and scooped her up, dragging her to safety.

"It's okay," Lucy whispered. "I've got you now."

Kelly didn't even glance at the girl. She stepped to the far side of the bed where the Japanese man had fallen, clawing at the blade jammed a full three inches into his arm.

He looked up and gasped, holding out his good hand.

"Please! I have money—"

"Spend it in Hell."

Kelly placed the muzzle between his eyes and pulled the trigger. The room erupted with the crack of the gun, and he fell back without a sound, most of the backside of his head missing.

Lucy held the sobbing girl, her frail body now wrapped in blood-splattered sheets, and she gently rocked her back and forth.

"It's okay. He's gone. You'll never be hurt again."

Lucy looked up and saw in Kelly's face a reflection of the anger she herself felt—a mindless, blazing rage.

"The third door," Lucy whispered. She didn't have to explain. She didn't have to say out loud what she already knew lay behind that steel door, and Kelly didn't need to hear it.

Without a word, the masked woman stepped back into the hallway, the gun held at her side.

43

"This way!" Maggie shouted as she dashed into the trees, leaping fallen logs and crashing through mud puddles like a deer on a run for its life. Reed followed, the rifle swinging from his hand as they hurtled down an invisible trail.

"How far?" he said.

"Not far. Half a mile, maybe."

Reed picked up his pace, pushing her from behind as Muddy Maggie led the way through the trees, heedless of pits or dangling tree limbs. He realized she knew this land like the back of her hand. She knew exactly where to go.

Five minutes later, they broke out of the woods, panting and stumbling onto slightly drier land. A small house with a slouching back porch loomed out of the shadows. Maggie ignored it and turned toward the water, beckoning Reed to follow. A small tin shed leaned next to the water as though it were only a breath of wind away from collapsing. Maggie paused at the door to input a combination into the lock, then snatched it off and undid the chain.

"Watch out for snakes!" she said as the door creaked open.

Reed cast a furtive glance around the interior of the shed as they slid inside. The small structure was no more than six feet wide and twice that deep, with an open back overhanging the water. A flat-bottomed metal boat sat on the bank, sheltered by the shed and chained off to a post. Maggie knelt to undo the lock, kicking a black snake out of the way as she did.

Reed recoiled, but the snake slithered into the water without striking.

"This is it?" he said, staring down at the rusty old boat and the dilapidated outboard motor hanging from the stern.

"I'm sorry. Does your family have a cigarette boat handy? My family is poor!"

Reed raised his hand, waving off her outburst as she hopped into the boat and moved toward the motor. He followed, pushing off from the bank and using the shed's wall to maneuver them toward open water. Maggie yanked on the motor's pull cord, and it coughed and whined but didn't start.

"There's not much gas," she said. "We'll have to be quick."

"Get me within three hundred yards. That's all I need."

The motor coughed again as Maggie pumped the primer bulb, then yanked the cable twice more. Dark exhaust spurted from the exposed propeller, and the motor rumbled to life.

Maggie shoved the foot of the outboard into the water.

"Let's ride!"

Reed knelt in the front of the boat, still cradling the rifle. Maggie twisted the throttle to max speed, and the nose of the boat rose just a little off the water as they rumbled away from the bank at twenty miles per hour.

"It's not enough, Maggie."

"I can't give you much more. It's an old boat!"

Maggie flipped the cover off the motor and grabbed the throttle directly, pressing it wide open with her thumb. The motor whined just a little louder, and they plowed through the rancid water.

"That's all she's got. Do you see anything?"

Reed squinted across the surface of the sleeping lake. As they moved away from the bank, the lake appeared much larger than it originally had, but no deeper. Stumps and pieces of rotting logs stuck up at random from the brackish water, but Maggie wove between them with practiced ease as she moved them back toward Gambit's lake house.

"I see them!" Reed pointed across the lake to a distant glimmer of reflective metal five hundred yards away. A bass boat, long and sleek with a big motor, had run afoul, and the right rear corner of the vessel was perched up out of the water at an awkward angle. Gambit's surviving goon was struggling to dislodge it from whatever they were grounded on, poking at the water with a canoe paddle.

"Take us in," Reed ordered, kneeling in the boat and bracing his right elbow against his right thigh. He lowered the rifle and squinted through the scope. The little boat hopped over an underwater obstacle—probably a rotting log or an alligator—and Reed almost pitched overboard. He caught himself on the boat's edge as Maggie called from the back.

"Remember! I need Gambit *alive*!"

Reed raised the rifle and gritted his teeth. After jamming a gun against David's skull, Gambit's fate was sealed. Maggie would have to interview a corpse.

Another tremor in the water, and Reed brought the crosshairs over the shoulder of the goon just as he saw Gambit's boat slide free of the obstruction and sink back into the water. The motor roared, and the boat's bow rose toward the sky, shooting forward far faster than Reed and Maggie's pursuit vessel.

Reed cursed and pivoted his sights away from the goon to the exposed bulk of the big outboard motor.

He placed his finger on the trigger as the boat shook beneath him. It was a two-hundred-yard shot, rapidly becoming a two-hundred-fifty-yard shot. He placed his finger on the trigger as the boat shook beneath him, took half a breath, held it, then squeezed.

Smoke trickled up from the outboard as it coughed and the nose of the lead boat slumped, but the vessel didn't stop. Gambit sat in the driver's seat, screaming at his goon as he turned his limping boat away from open water and toward the closest bank fifty yards away.

The goon stumbled to the back of the boat and raised his assault rifle, but before he could fire, his forehead exploded under Reed's next shot. Gambit ducked beneath the bulkhead, steering himself directly toward shore.

Maggie turned to follow, closing the gap between the two boats as Gambit's vessel crashed into the soft mud of the bank. A burst of automatic gunfire erupted toward them, and Reed and Maggie ducked as bullets whistled overhead.

Reed knew it was only cover fire and that Gambit was making a last desperate attempt to disappear into the woods. Reed lifted his head above the side of the boat and saw Gambit stumbling into the trees, dragging David Montgomery behind him. A pistol glinted in Gambit's left hand, and Reed raised the rifle.

In the clear moonlight, he saw Gambit look over his shoulder as the crosshairs descended over his face. Reed sighted in on the base of Gambit's neck, then wrapped his finger around the trigger and pressed it home.

The pistol cracked only a millisecond before the rifle did. Both Gambit and David crumpled to the ground, and blood erupted into the air like a geyser. Reed felt the boat's nose scrape bottom, and he jumped out, rushing up the bank. Maggie shouted for him not to shoot, but it didn't matter. Long before Reed made it to the two bodies, he knew one thing for certain— neither man would ever stand again.

Gambit lay on the mud with his face turned skyward, a hole the size of an orange blown through his neck. The dying light in his eyes faded into darkness as Reed slid to his knees next to the two bodies.

David Montgomery lay across Gambit's legs, his face twisted in agony as blood bubbled up from the bullet hole in his ribcage. He looked at Reed with confusion, pain, and so much fear.

Reed dropped the rifle and scooped his father out of the muck, pulling him close to his chest as the sobs came. There was no stopping them—no checking them. His chest shook, and he cried like he hadn't cried since he was a small child.

"Dad . . . Dad, it's Reed. I'm here. Don't go . . ."

David's head twisted toward the sound. Reed heard the soft footfalls of Maggie just behind him, but he didn't look up. He stared into David's eyes and saw the dark clouds of a mind driven into insanity—no recognition, no humanity, just pure biology, as if David's body were a house and nobody was home.

Reed clutched him closer, then fumbled to find the wound, trying to block the flow of blood. But there was no use. Even if he could stop the bleeding, Reed could tell by the trail of blood exiting David's mouth that at least one lung was cut, not to mention other vital organs.

Reed gripped David's hand.

"Dad, it's me. Please, don't go before you see me."

David's gaze fixated on Reed, shadows crossing behind it, still without recognition.

"Dad, it's your son, Reed. We were motorheads together. The car, Dad. Don't you remember?"

David coughed and sprayed blood across Reed's chest. His breaths were growing weaker, less frequent. Reed could feel the cold touch of death seeping into David's hands. He blinked, then a strange light passed across his face, and the faintest hint of a smile tugged at this lips.

"The car . . ." His hoarse voice was barely audible, so Reed leaned in close. David swallowed blood, then his lips parted again.

"The car . . . trusts you."

An overwhelming rush of longing surged through Reed's core as he bent forward and hugged his father close. David Montgomery remembered. Almost two decades had passed since that moment in the garage when Reed first nursed an old car to life. Those had been his father's words that day: "The car trusts you."

Reed sobbed, rocking back and forth as he felt the last warmth of life fade from David's body, his soul vanishing into the night. His breath stopped, but the memories remained, his last whispered words sending a stronger message than an entire speech ever could have.

"The car trusts you."

David Montgomery remembered.

44

Banks sat in the bed and rocked the girl for the best part of an hour. After untying her and wrapping her in the warmth of a clean blanket, she hugged her and whispered soft words.

The little girl cried, shook, and sobbed, and she buried her face in Banks's chest while the blood of the dead man on the floor grew cold and began to dry. In the heat of the moment, Banks had done something she never imagined herself capable of—she had brutally killed somebody, driving two loads of buckshot through his body.

But in the context of this broken, weeping girl, Banks didn't care. She almost wished she could do it again, more brutally this time, by pressing her foot on his throat and breaking his neck.

Banks kissed the top of the girl's head and rubbed her back.

"What's your name, sweetheart?"

When the girl spoke, it was in a heavy Eastern European accent. "Polina."

Banks smiled, gently brushing the tears away from her face, then she squeezed her hand.

"Well, Polina, I want you to know something. I know you're hurt, but you aren't broken. You're strong. You're a survivor. Never forget that."

Polina buried her head in Banks's chest.

It was another hour before Banks tucked Polina into the bed. The girl fell asleep with no regard for the dead man on the floor. Banks thought it was probably better if she moved her to another room, but she wasn't sure what else was happening in the house, and she wanted to find out first. As soon as Polina collapsed into an exhausted, traumatized sleep, Banks picked up the shotgun and walked back across the room, taking the squeaking steps one at a time to the ground floor.

The bottom of the house was completely illuminated now. The fat man lay in the kitchen, decapitated in the midst of the largest pool of blood Banks had ever seen. Wolfgang leaned over the counter, sorting through a stack of cameras, computers, and other electronic equipment. Kelly stood near the window overlooking the lake, her mask removed and her distorted features staring out over the water in icy silence.

As Banks entered, Wolfgang stared at her a moment, glanced down at the shotgun, then looked back at the stack of electronics.

"It was a blackmail operation," he said. "There's an entire brothel downstairs. Two rooms were used for under-aged sex by wealthy businessmen, celebrities, politicians . . . whoever. There was an office under the second-floor staircase that housed the recording equipment. I found thumb drives labeled with a lot of big names, but I haven't watched them."

"Don't," Banks said flatly.

Wolfgang nodded and set a camera down on the counter. The stairwell to the basement creaked, and Lucy appeared. Kelly looked up immediately, her eyes shooting a question.

Lucy nodded once. "They're asleep. Most of them required sedation. I found some sleeping pills in the kitchen."

"*They?*" Banks asked.

Lucy's gaze fell to the floor. "There's an entire line of prison cells beneath the kitchen. Four girls . . . all fifteen or less."

Banks felt a wave of sickness and overwhelming rage. Suddenly, her skin felt hot, and she rushed to the counter, picking up an open bottle of water and draining it. When she set it down and looked around the room, the others were avoiding each other's gazes, trying to find peace in a bit of wall or carpet.

Banks's hand shook, and she swallowed. "Where is Reed's father?"

Kelly grunted. "The guys from the SUV ran out the back just as you two were carving up the fat guy. David was with them."

Wolfgang nodded. "Right after I stopped the cover fire, I heard some shots from the backyard. My guess is that Reed was in the woods with a rifle. Maybe he ran them down. Hard to say."

Silence lapsed over the room again, seconds ticking into minutes. And then, for the first time, Kelly was the one to break it. She turned away from the window and faced them, her arms crossed, her distorted features twisted into an even more hideous snarl.

"Whatever it takes, wherever they are . . . I'm going to run the bastards responsible for this into the ground, and I'm going to carve them apart, one piece at a time. If these are the people Reed is at war with, I'm at war with them, too."

Banks saw Lucy's and Wolfgang's rage, the amazing horror of what they had seen, and their burning desire for vengeance.

She turned back to Kelly. "We all are."

45

Reed and Maggie scooped a shallow grave in the lakeside, using the paddle and a small bucket from Gambit's boat. It took over an hour, but eventually, it was deep enough to safely protect David from scavengers until he could be afforded a proper burial. They lifted his broken body and laid him down in the mud.

Reed stood for a long moment at the foot of the grave, staring at his father. In a way, David Montgomery looked more peaceful in this moment than he had since that fateful day decades before when he and Reed worked together on the old Camaro. There was something in his face that radiated rest, even through the cold pallor of death. It was as though he had been at war with something or somebody for years, and now, after all that time, he was free.

Reed knelt and gently scooped earth over his father's face. After a moment, Maggie joined in, and ten minutes later, the hole was filled and packed down, hard enough to ensure that the next Louisiana rain wouldn't wash the topsoil away.

A hot breeze blew in over the lake. As Reed glanced toward the water, he could see nothing on the far shore. The lights of the house, like the bodies that lay next to him, were now prisoners of the swamp.

"Will anyone have heard the gunshots?" he asked.

Maggie shrugged. "This isn't really a tourist destination. Locals might mark it off as gator hunters or rednecks."

Reed nodded slowly, then settled down onto the damp earth and pulled his knees to chin level. He doubted that gator hunters used automatic weapons, but he wasn't going to worry about that right now. Maggie settled down beside him, and the song of the swamp wind filled their ears, drowning out the memory of the gunshots and the screams.

"Gambit's dead," Maggie said after a while.

"I'm sorry. I had no choice."

Maggie shrugged. "I guess I should be happy. The threat's gone."

Reed drew in a long breath, then shook his head. "No, I'm afraid it's not. Gambit wasn't a boss. He was an underling. A buffer man."

"So, you still think this is some kind of conspiracy?"

Reed nodded. "Without a doubt. And Aiden Phillips is at the top of it all."

Maggie picked at the mud with a stick, scratching various patterns into it.

"I never got to tell you, but I think Robert Coulier was Gambit's replacement for me. My secretary of state has undergone a 'mental breakdown,' whatever that means. My guess is that he's either far greater a wimp than I thought, or Coulier somehow got to him. With him out of the way, Coulier takes the executive office."

"You're not dead," Reed said. "You can go back now and take over."

Maggie poked at the mud, her shoulders slumped.

Reed heard a soft sob escape her lips and was surprised to see her shoulders shake. She didn't cry, but her body wanted her to.

Hesitantly, he placed a hand on her shoulder and gave it a soft squeeze.

When she looked up, her eyes were red but not wet.

"My god, Reed. I never imagined I was signing up for something like this. I just wanted to make the state a better place. I wanted to lead. I wanted to be a hero."

Reed squeezed her shoulder again, then withdrew his hand. "It doesn't take a hero to lead men into battle. It takes a hero to be one of those men who goes into battle."

Maggie squinted at him. "Who said that?"

Reed offered a weary laugh. "Some Army guy. Only Army guys have time to come up with things like that. Marines are too busy getting the job done."

Maggie returned the laugh.

"The important thing is, it's true. You could've settled for making the state a better place—lowering taxes, building schools . . . whatever governors do. Instead, you went into battle and did what nobody before you was willing to do. Whatever you've done, whatever it costs, you took the risk and put yourself on the line for your people. That makes you a hero in my book . . . for whatever my book is worth."

Maggie nodded slowly. "Thank you. That actually means a lot."

The moon shone down over them, bathing the lakeside in cool blue light. Even though it was hot, and the water stank, and the mud had oozed into all kinds of uncomfortable places, Reed couldn't help but think that this was the most peace he had felt in a long time. There was still so much uncertainty in his life. He'd literally just buried his father. Someplace across the lake, Banks was with the others, and she was hurting and alone and probably very confused by their last encounter.

He didn't know if she could ever love him after everything he had done —the bodies, the gunfire, the endless wreckage that now followed her life as much as his. In that context, kissing the governor seemed a small atrocity, yet it felt like his biggest betrayal. He didn't know if she could forgive that. He didn't know if he could ask her to.

But what he did know was that he loved Banks more than he'd ever loved any woman. And he also knew that the breath of the wind on the water was no more than the calm before the final storm.

"What are you going to do now, Reed Montgomery?"

Reed picked himself up and dusted the mud off his knees. "First, I'm going to do something about those bodies, then I'm going to take you back to the city where you can make your own decisions. And then . . ."

He cast one more glance at the lake. Something cold and angry boiled in his stomach—the kind of burning resolve that saturated his bones and galvanized him into action, no matter if that action cost him everything.

"And then I'm going to hunt down Aiden Phillips, and I'm going to prosecute him like no judge or jury ever will."

Maggie stood up and placed a hand on Reed's shoulder. There was iron in her grip—the strength of a woman who had been pushed to the brink of Hell and was now about to push back.

"Leave the bodies for the gators, Reed. I'm with you."

DEATH CYCLE
THE REED MONTGOMERY SERIES Book 6

When brute force isn't enough, desperate men make desperate choices.

Elite assassin Reed Montgomery has set his sights on his greatest enemy—the sadistic criminal mastermind, Aiden Phillips. Surrounded by a team of vigilantes as ruthless and determined as himself, Reed only needs to know where to strike.

An orchestrated encounter with a shadowy informant gives Reed the information he needs: The secrets to bringing Aiden down lie in rural Colombia, where the heart of Aiden's operation beats in secret.

Reed is ready and willing to carry his war across international borders, but the jungles of Colombia are a dark and violent place, and Aiden will unleash hell to protect his empire.

As everything spins out of control, Reed refuses to take his foot off the gas.

He'll destroy Aiden . . . or die trying.

Get your copy today at
severnriverbooks.com/series/reed-montgomery

ABOUT THE AUTHOR

Logan Ryles was born in small town USA and knew from an early age he wanted to be a writer. After working as a pizza delivery driver, sawmill operator, and banker, he finally embraced the dream and has been writing ever since. With a passion for action-packed and mystery-laced stories, Logan's work has ranged from global-scale political thrillers to small town vigilante hero fiction.

Beyond writing, Logan enjoys saltwater fishing, road trips, sports, and fast cars. He lives with his wife and three fun-loving dogs in Alabama.

Sign up for Logan Ryles's reader list at
severnriverbooks.com/authors/logan-ryles

Printed in the United States
by Baker & Taylor Publisher Services